CHAPTER 1

Dr. Amanda Garvas stopped her rental car in the middle of the deserted Montana highway. Her cell phone stubbornly refused to provide any service, and the map spread out on her passenger seat kept sending her on scenic routes that continually missed her destination.

"Yep, I'm lost," she finally admitted out loud.

What a ridiculously long day it had been. Amanda had left Seattle at 8:00 that morning, only to sit on the tarmac for three hours as they waited for the fog to clear. Once she finally made it to Boise, she discovered that she'd missed her connecting flight to Great Falls, Montana, forcing her to spend another two hours waiting on standby for a later flight.

When she finally stepped off the plane in Montana, it was to discover that the rental car company had lost her reservation. After another 30 minutes of begging and praying, they finally found her a vehicle. Only for her to get stuck out here in the Montana wilds, with the first orange hints of sunset reminding her that it would soon be dark.

Lord, I could use some help, she thought. *Not that I don't want to stay out tonight with the coyotes and wolves. I'm sure they're great.*

Almost as in answer, she heard the long call of a wolf in the distance. It was enough to get her moving. She wasn't sure which direction was Highland Canyon, but whatever kept her moving away from the wolves was enough for her.

"What I wouldn't give for a hotel right now," she muttered.

Fifteen minutes later, Amanda passed a highway marker that she'd overlooked before. She hit the brakes and spread the map across the steering wheel. She thought that number sounded familiar.

"Yes!" she breathed. This was the turn that should take her in to Highland Canyon. She crossed her fingers and followed the new road.

Within ten minutes she was rewarded with the sight of a small town ahead of her. With dusk falling all around now, she'd never been so grateful to see civilization.

She double-checked the address of her destination. It should be on the main road, somewhere close by. Then she saw a sign attached to a pretty brick building, "Dr. Daniel Shane, Pediatrics."

She pulled her car into a dirt parking space in front of the building, relieved to have finally made it. Shifting her car into park, she leaned forward to peer through her window. Then she squinted her eyes in the low light, wondering if she was seeing things correctly.

Amanda had worked in several facilities during her time as a practicing doctor and even more since she left medicine to work at the Weisman Trust, a foundation that gave financial grants to nonprofits. But in all her experience, she'd never seen a doctor's office that looked quite so... fun.

Healed in Him

Maggie Bennett

CONTENTS

The building itself looked like it used to be someone's home and had since been converted to an office. There were several dormer windows along the roofline, and it had an old-fashioned raised front porch that ran the width of the house. Amanda could imagine the original homeowners loading it down with rocking chairs and friendly town gossip, but that wasn't how the porch was being used anymore.

Amanda smiled as she surveyed the several kid-sized slides that extended from the porch to the ground below. There was a climbing rope hanging from each corner of the porch ceiling, and the office's brick wall had been dotted with plastic handles that converted the entire face of the building to a climbing rock wall. There was even a set of monkey bars that ran where a railing would have typically been.

If she'd been here earlier in the day, Amanda could only assume the makeshift playground would be swarming with kids. It certainly looked inviting enough.

She walked up the porch steps, brushing past one lone porch swing, presumably there for parents to have a comfortable seat while their children played. She paused at the front door, uttering a silent prayer that everything would go well. She needed this grant to work. All her plans depended on it.

Amanda straightened her tailored suit jacket over her simple silk blouse, trying to ignore how rumpled she must look after her insane travel day. She smoothed her straight dark hair as best as she could and then tried the door. She was relieved to find it was still unlocked.

She entered a quiet waiting room. No one was working the front desk, which was hardly surprising given the hour.

"Hello?" she called.

"One minute," she heard a cheerful, deep voice respond from somewhere down the hall. "Be right there."

Amanda turned back from the desk and surveyed the room around her. She saw that the fun atmosphere of the front porch had been carried inside, as the waiting room was filled with books and toys. She made a mental note to include the playful feel of the office in her report. The Trust's Board of Directors would surely like that. You never knew what little detail would be enough to make the difference between funding and a denial.

"Sorry to keep you waiting," the same voice said behind her. "How can I help you?"

Amanda turned as she spoke. "Funny you should say that. I'm the one who should – " She broke off as she found herself staring into a set of gorgeous dark brown eyes with golden flecks.

She adjusted her focus and registered that the brown eyes belonged to the friendly face of a man who was surely the doctor she'd come to meet. He wore a white lab coat over a set of broad shoulders with a stethoscope sticking out of the pocket. His sandy brown hair looked mussed, as if he'd run his hands through it recently, and he had an open, pleasant face with an adorably crooked nose.

Granted, that face looked slightly confused now at the way she'd stopped in the middle of her sentence. She cleared her throat and continued, "I'm the one who should apologize to you. For keeping you waiting." She took a deep breath and tried to clear her head. "I'm Dr. Amanda Garvas. I think you probably expected me several hours ago."

"Ah." Recognition showed in his eyes. He held out his hand, which Amanda took in a firm shake. "I'm glad that you made it. I was worried about you. I called the Trust to make sure you were still coming, but they didn't know where you were either."

"I'll have to call them and let them know I'm here," said Amanda. "As soon as I get this darn cell phone to work."

"Good news," he said. "Your phone should work in town. It's only along the highways outside of Highland Canyon that everyone loses service." He clapped his hands together. "Well, as I'm sure you've guessed, I'm Dr. Shane, though I hope you'll call me Daniel. I'm glad you were able to come visit, Dr. Garvas."

"Amanda, please."

"Amanda. Welcome to my practice. I'm very excited about this."

"Me too," Amanda said, trying to concentrate more on her professional role and less on his eyes. "I love visiting potential grantees. I hope we're able to find a way for the Weisman Trust to help you with your facility expansion."

Daniel flashed a brilliant smile at her. "I'm hope so, too. I've been planning this new clinic for the better part of two years now. It's very encouraging to be so close to seeing it happen." He leaned back against the counter. "I admit I'm new at this," he continued. "Where do we go from here? I'd be happy to give you a tour of the office, but I get the feeling you've had a rough travel day."

Amanda laughed. "The roughest. So, while yes, I would normally jump on a tour, I would appreciate putting this one off until tomorrow morning. I'll be in town all week, so we've got plenty of time."

"I understand," he said. "I can't stand travelling. I do everything I can to stay right here."

"Including building a state-of-the-art medical clinic right here in town?"

He laughed. "I guess so."

Amanda smiled at him. "I'll swing by bright and early tomorrow, and we can get started. You can show me around, I'll shadow you with some patients – assuming it's ok with them, of course – and then we can get into some of the nitty gritty details of the new clinic in the afternoon. Sound good?"

Daniel grinned again, something that Amanda was starting to realize he did very easily. "Sounds excellent. We open at 8:00."

"I'll be here." She gathered herself together and turned for the door. "Now I just need to find my hotel. It can't be harder than finding this town."

Daniel followed her. "I assume you're staying at the Ten Trees Inn?"

"Um," Amanda glanced through her bag to find the hotel reservation that her assistant had printed out for her. "Yes, I am. " She looked up. "How'd you know?"

"Lucky guess. It's the only hotel in town." He reached around her to pull the door open and held it as she walked through. He followed her onto the porch, saying, "And I've got a little more good news for you." He put a hand on each of her arms and pivoted her slightly to face diagonally across the street before letting go. Amanda swallowed, affected despite herself at the brief contact. Daniel pointed to a building across the road. "There's your hotel. No getting lost."

Amanda breathed a sigh of relief. She wouldn't even have to get back into the car. *Thank you, Jesus*, she thought.

Daniel walked with her down the steps. "Leave your car here," he said. "I'll help you with your bags."

"Thanks." She popped the trunk, and Daniel easily swung her small suitcase up into his arms.

"After you."

As they crossed the street, Amanda couldn't help but notice that Daniel kept glancing at her curiously.

Amanda blushed and squirmed inwardly as he appeared to study her. Did she have something on her face? She thought ruefully of the chocolate croissant she'd enjoyed on the long drive from Great Falls, back before she got lost and became too stressed to eat. She could only pray that she wasn't wearing the chocolate now.

"Sorry," he said after a moment, "but at the risk of sounding clichéd, I really think I've met you before."

Amanda was flooded with relief. No chocolate smear on her then. "Well, it's possible, I suppose. I do a fair bit of traveling for work."

Daniel shook his head. "No," he said slowly. "I don't think it was recent. Where did you grow up?"

"Seattle," said Amanda. She gave a small smile. "I haven't strayed too far from home."

"Nothing wrong with that. But that's not it." They'd reached the hotel, a quaint, simple inn that looked inviting. Daniel set down the suitcase and once more held open the door for her. "Where'd you do your residency?"

"Northwest Hospital," she said, passing into the lobby.

"Medical school?" He followed her in, dropping her suitcase by the front desk.

"Washington State." She rang a small bell on the counter to summon an attendant.

Daniel snapped his fingers. "That's it! I do know you! You worked with Dr. Kowalski, didn't you?"

Amanda's mouth dropped open. "Ruth Kowalski? Of course! She's the best child life specialist in the northwest."

"At least the country," said Daniel, gesturing wide with his hands.

Amanda grinned. "Glad to know you feel the same way I do. But how do you know her?"

"I met Dr. Kowalski at a seminar a few years ago in Boise. She was presenting on the role of play in promoting recovery rates. So many doctors ignore that side of care; it was refreshing to see someone take a holistic view of pediatric medicine."

He went on, his face alive with enthusiasm. "I was so impressed with her that I introduced myself to her after the presentation and asked if I could pick her brain on a few cases. She generously agreed, and I repaid her kindness by latching on to her as a mentor with a stranglehold." He laughed. "She's probably sick of me, but I won't let her go. She keeps threatening me that she's going to retire and force me find a new mentor."

Amanda remembered watching Dr. Kowalski in the classroom. "She really is something. She definitely helped expand my viewpoint during medical school beyond the traditional approaches."

"I bet."

A young female attendant was at the desk now, and Amanda spent the next few moments checking in. She turned to Daniel once she had her key in hand.

"But you never explained how you knew that *I* worked with Dr. Kowalski."

"Ah, yes," said Daniel. "At that presentation where I first met her, she included a video of some of her students working with young cancer patients, and I specifically remember you. You were explaining to a child what chemo was and how it was going to make her feel."

Amanda laughed. "Oh no! That was my starving student phase! I probably had dirty scrubs and frizzy hair."

"I don't remember a bit of that." He smiled. "But I do remember how compassionate you seemed. It really stuck with me."

Amanda flushed. "Thank you. I'm glad to know some good came out of that. I remember being very nervous when Dr. Kowalski first mentioned that she wanted to film us practicing her techniques." She frowned. "What is she doing now, anyways?"

"She's still at the medical school. Last time we talked, she was taking over the student internship placements. I'm sure you know better than most how hands-on she likes to be."

Amanda nodded. "She really does."

The two smiled at each other and fell into a comfortable silence. With that short conversation, Amanda felt she was looking at a friend rather than a new acquaintance.

"Well," said Daniel, "I'll leave you to settle in. Looking forward to work tomorrow."

"Me, too," said Amanda, truly meaning it. "Thanks for walking me."

She watched him stride back across the street to his office. After a moment, she turned to find the hotel attendant watching her with an amused smile.

Amanda straightened up. She gathered her suitcase and headed for the rooms, trying to ignore the knowing look she was leaving behind.

AFTER UNLOADING her luggage in her room, Amanda ventured out again in search of food. After that day's never-ending car ride, she was famished, and she'd noticed a diner located conveniently next door to the hotel.

Walking through the restaurant's swinging doors, Amanda couldn't help but be surprised. She'd expected typical small-town diner décor, but was instead met with a room that felt like a cross between an old-fashioned library and a hall of mirrors. Wood paneling lined the bottom half of the walls, while mirrors covered the top. The two surfaces combined gave a feeling of having sturdy ground under your feet while still being surrounded by open skies. It was a pleasant, if unexpected, combination, and Amanda couldn't stop herself from smiling as she surveyed the room. The place was clearly a local hangout, filled with people enjoying their dinners while talking with each across the different tables.

Amanda felt slightly out of place as her business suit stuck out in a sea of jeans and cowboys hats. She quietly ordered the pot roast to-go from a waiter posted behind the dark mahogany bar, and then settled in as she waited, letting the friendly chatter from the room wash over her and help ease her tension from the long travel day.

A red-haired petite woman brought out the food to her.

"One pot roast for Amanda," she said. "I take it you're Amanda?"

"That's me." Amanda took the food and inhaled the intoxicating scent. "Oh, thank you."

"You're welcome," the woman said brightly as Amanda turned to go. "I hope you'll come back by while you're in town."

Amanda stopped. "You know I'm a visitor?" she asked.

The woman smiled and nodded.

"I guess this town's so small that you know everyone, huh?" Amanda went on. "You can probably spot a visitor a mile away."

The waitress smiled. "Not exactly." With a mischievous grin, she reached out and pulled something off Amanda's sleeve. It was the barcode sticker the airline placed on her checked luggage earlier that morning.

"This gave you away," the woman said with a laugh. She crumpled the sticker in her hands and tossed it into a trashcan by the hostess station.

Amanda blushed. "Oh. I guess I picked that up by accident." Inwardly she cringed. Had that been stuck to her when she met Daniel? With her late arrival and wrinkled clothes, the sticker was the last nail in the coffin of her professionalism.

Amanda sighed. Nothing she could do about it now. "Well, you're right," she said to the waitress. "I'm from Seattle."

"What brings you to Highland Canyon?"

"Business," said Amanda. "I'm working with one of your local healthcare providers. Do you know Dr. Shane?"

"Know him?" asked the woman, her eyes brightening. "I love him. He's done so much for my daughter."

"Really?" asked Amanda.

She nodded. "But almost everyone in this town will tell you the same. He's a marvel."

Just then, the waitress turned her head, distracted by some patrons waving her down.

"I'd better run," she said, turning back to Amanda. "Enjoy that dinner. And come back by when you can. Ask for Millie."

"Will do," said Amanda, enjoying the friendly atmosphere of the diner. "And thanks."

Amanda brought the food back to her room and immediately traded her business suit for pajamas and a pair of fuzzy socks. She settled into her comfy hotel bed, incredibly grateful to be in a clean room rather than still out in the wilds. She was about to dig into her take-out when her phone rang.

Amanda let out a small groan when she read the caller ID. "Beth Weisman." Of course her boss was calling to check up on her.

"Hey, Beth," she said, injecting a perky tone into her voice that she didn't quite feel. "What's up?"

"Ah, Amanda. I wanted to make sure you'd made it. Dr. Shane called earlier in the day because you weren't there yet."

"Are you still at the office?"

"Yes, it's been a crazy day. Lots of work still to get through." Amanda could picture Beth sitting at her desk. Her salt-and-pepper hair would be pulled back in her standard bun, and she was probably twirling her pen in her fingers like she always did when she was on a phone call.

"Well, don't work too hard."

"Uh huh." Beth said absently. "Speaking of working, I assume you are now in Highland Canyon? Have you conducted your initial site visit yet?"

"Yeah, about that. Unfortunately, I didn't manage much of an inspection because…" Amanda closed her eyes, not wanting to relive her nightmare of a day. "Let's just say that my travel plans did not go according to schedule. I didn't make it here until Dr. Shane's office was closed. But we're going to start first thing tomorrow morning."

Beth sighed over the line. "Ok, but please make sure you're taking this seriously. This is a very big grant, both for the Trust and for your career."

Amanda didn't need her boss to remind her of that fact. When she'd walked away from medicine over a year ago, the grants officer position at the Weisman Trust had appeared like a lifeline. With her background as a doctor, she was a natural fit for the foundation that specialized in grants to healthcare nonprofits, and, even better, it got her out of clinical work that had become too emotionally painful. In the time since, she'd worked on progressively larger grant projects, checking out potential grantees and what sort of impact each could have. None of them had been as big as this project though.

"I am taking it seriously, Beth. Very. A grant this size is not something I take lightly."

"I know you don't," said Beth, and Amanda was glad to hear that she sounded satisfied. "This is a big one, to be basically starting a new clinic from scratch, and I'm a little skittish about it. You've got to be my eyes and ears on the ground and determine if it's a good use of funds. You're one of my best officers, though, and I know you'll be fine."

"Thanks, Beth," said Amanda, trying to feel grateful instead of annoyed by Beth constantly checking up on her. Given her relative inexperience in the field, she'd half expected Beth to insist on coming on this trip with her, so the fact that Amanda was able to come by herself was a victory.

"And don't forget," continued Beth, "there's that major gifts officer position that's opening up next month. Close this grant, and I'll have no problem recommending you to the Board for that job."

Amanda closed her eyes. She really wanted that promotion. No, she corrected herself, she needed it. It would validate her choice to leave medicine behind.

She knew that Beth could convince the Board to do anything, whether it was to award a certain grant or hire a specific person. She had to impress her.

"So what's Dr. Shane like?" Beth was asking.

Amanda hesitated, picking her words carefully. If she'd been chatting to a friend, she might have admitted that she found him charming. That wouldn't work for this conversation though. She remembered one of the first rules drilled into her head at the Trust – no dating between Trust employees and potential grantees. Beth had explained how romantic relations could ruin the objectivity that a grant officer had to maintain in order to make the best recommendations. So the last thing Amanda could tell Beth now was that Daniel Shane was funny, open, and had a way of grinning that distracted Amanda completely.

Instead, she retreated into the standard words and phrases she'd picked up during her year at the organization. "I think he's very open to my visit and ready to partner with the Trust. He seems a tad... unorthodox. He's got a really unique feel going on in the office that I expect his patients love." As a matter of fact, she suspected that his patients probably loved *him* as much as they loved the fun playground equipment, but she wasn't quite ready to go into that with Beth yet. "I think this could be an excellent investment." There, that sounded good.

"That's great," said Beth. "Can't wait to read your notes on the site visit. Why don't you call me again after you've spent some time at the office?"

"Sure," said Amanda, barely stopping herself from rolling her eyes. Couldn't she go one day without a check-in call?

"Ok, I'm going to let you go then. Keep me updated." Beth hung up abruptly as was her usual custom.

"Bye," Amanda said to herself. She threw her phone down and leaned to the bedside table where she'd stashed that evening's dinner. "And hello to you," she sighed as she opened the Styrofoam container.

Amanda murmured a quick prayer before digging in to her meal. She closed her eyes in bliss as she enjoyed her first bite of tender roast, finally relaxing after her day. Though she hadn't said as much to Beth, Amanda felt nervous about this visit, and it wasn't just the nerve-wracking time she'd had getting here.

Amanda had spent the last year putting distance from her time as an active doctor. She'd known it wouldn't be easy starting over in a new field at the age of 30, but even she was surprised by the challenges she'd faced adjusting to life outside of the medical arena. Now that she finally had good prospects in her new career, she desperately wanted to make a success of it. Successfully shepherding a major grant would do a lot towards proving to herself that she'd made the right choice to leave medicine.

And if that grant happened also to help the handsome doctor she'd met that evening, then that was all to the good.

CHAPTER 2

Daniel pulled his rolling chair up to his battered old desk. He'd salvaged the furniture years ago as a poor med school student from the side of the road. Nowadays, his nurses frequently teased him about it. They said he should get a desk that didn't "look like a hobo shelter," but he couldn't. He loved the desk because he felt it reminded him never to get too uppity. He rubbed his hands across the weathered surface, thinking that it's hard to feel like a hotshot know-everything doctor when you're using a desk that has "Sand Creek Plumbing" stamped on it.

Daniel ran through the events of the previous evening in his mind. Although it had been so late when Amanda finally arrived, he still felt they'd gotten off to a good start. When he'd first seen her, he was a little stunned. She was younger than Daniel had expected – about his age, he guessed – and her striking cosmopolitan style and beautiful face looked out of place in his little country practice. Once he got over his surprise, however, he'd found her to be intelligent and friendly. He was rather looking forward to working with her.

That connection through Dr. Kowalski was definitely handy. He hoped it would help build his credibility with Amanda and make it more likely that she'd recommend the grant. From what he gathered of the process, he needed to convince Amanda that the new clinic was needed, and, assuming that worked, she'd recommend the project to her boss. Daniel got the impression that once the boss approved, the grant was a go.

Speaking of Dr. Kowalski, Daniel had the feeling that his mentor would be excited to hear about one of her former students. He opened up his email and started a new message to her. "You're never going to guess who walked into my office yesterday…" he wrote.

After sending off the news that Amanda was in Highland Canyon, Daniel saw a new message pop up from his pastor. He knew what it was before he even opened it. It was an invitation to attend a men's Bible study group, one he'd received and ignored before. He sighed as he hit "delete." Sure, he'd love to pause and study God's word, but where was he supposed to find the time? He had to complete this project and open the new facility. He gently touched the framed picture on top of his old desk of two twin babies. He had to do it for them.

He heard the front door chime. Showtime. He jumped up from his chair and strode back out to the main lobby.

Just like the evening before, there was Amanda coming through the door. Daniel dimly registered in the back of his mind that he hadn't imagined it – she really was a lovely woman. Built on the petite side, she probably didn't even come up to his chin. This morning, she'd pulled her dark hair back in a low bun, revealing fresh glowing skin and bright green eyes that arrested his attention.

"Good morning, Daniel," she said as soon as she saw him, repeating her cordial handshake of the evening before. "Ready to get started today?"

"Very," said Daniel, liking the combination of her steady grip paired with the faint scent of lilacs that she carried on the air. "I've arranged for a slightly lesser load of patients today so we'll have time to go over the project, but we've still got plenty of people coming in to give you a taste of what we do."

"Super." They both turned as the door chimed again.

"And here's part of my crew," said Daniel as two of his nurses came through the door to start their daily shifts. "Guys, please meet Dr. Garvas of the Weisman Trust."

As Amanda greeted and chatted with the nurses, Daniel stood back and watched. This woman was the final key to starting the new clinic, something he felt God had been calling him to do for two years. To be so close was exhilarating, but, looking at Amanda's intelligent eyes, he had a feeling that the deal was far from closed. He needed to make a good impression this week.

The first of his patients started coming through the door, always the favorite part of Daniel's day. He went out first to give a fist bump to ten-year-old Grant who had a cast on his foot. He'd earned it by jumping off the school monkey bars and landing poorly.

"Looking good, buddy," he said. "That cast might be coming off today!" He turned to Grant's mother and smiled. "I'm sure you'll be glad of that, too."

She rolled her eyes toward the ceiling. "You have no idea! If I have to wrestle a plastic bag over that foot so he can shower one more time, I am going to lose it."

"Hi, Dr. Shane," said a small voice. He looked down to see a sweet four-year-old named Maddie. He squatted down beside her.

"Maddie Donaldson, is it really time for your check-up again?" She bobbed her head delightedly. "Then you must have had a birthday!"

"I did!" she squealed. "I turned four. And we had a clown."

"So cool!" He gave her a high-five, then stood and turned back to the front desk. He was momentarily disconcerted to find Amanda watching him with a slight smile on her face. The nurses had apparently left to begin to check in patients.

"Sorry about that." His mouth twitched. "I find clowns very exciting."

Amanda nodded solemnly. "Totally get that."

He laughed. "Shall we?"

"After you."

The morning passed very quickly. Daniel brought Amanda into all of his consults, after first getting the patients' consent to have an additional doctor in the room. He noticed she was fairly hands-off and content to watch. In every appointment, she told the patient to pretend she wasn't there, which surprised him somewhat. She obviously was a trained clinician; anyone who'd worked with Dr. Kowalski would be. But she seemed to have no interest in interacting with patients now. Maybe it was because they weren't her patients. Or maybe that was something that a grant officer just didn't do, even a medically trained one. Daniel really wasn't sure.

Amanda made notes throughout the appointments, but for the life of him, Daniel couldn't tell if she was writing good things or bad. He tried to keep his mind on his work and not worry about it, but it wasn't completely possible to keep from wondering.

In between patients, Daniel showed Amanda around his practice. He was impressed by the intelligent questions she asked him.

"From how far away do you expect to draw patients?" she'd asked on one such occasion.

"Oh, I'd say from within a 100 mile radius. We're fairly isolated out here, and the surrounding towns are even more lacking in medical facilities than we are."

Her eyebrows rose, and she followed up with several more questions. "Do you feel that you can keep up with the increased patient load, drawing from so far away? Will the facility be large enough for it? How many surgical suites will be included? What about the wear and tear on your equipment with so many patients? Do you have money in the budget for increased maintenance if your population estimates are low?" And so on. It was all Daniel could do to answer as best he could before the next question came along. She was certainly going to keep him on his toes.

When lunch rolled around, Daniel was glad to sit down over one of the fresh turkey sandwiches he'd had brought in for the staff.

"Why don't we eat at my desk?" Daniel suggested to Amanda. "We can continue our conversation in there."

In his office, Daniel offered his rolling chair to Amanda, which she gracefully accepted. He settled into his visitor chair and started on his lunch.

Amanda ran her finger over the carvings on his desk. "Sand Creek Plumbing?" she read.

He sighed. "I have an unconventional past."

"Sure, you do," she said, unable to completely hide a smile. She flipped open her notebook beside her plate. "Ok, let's talk staffing. You're the only doctor here, right?"

"Right."

"Have you ever thought of taking on a partner?"

"Not really. That would mean relinquishing some control, and I suppose I've got my own definite ideas of how I want to run things."

Truthfully, Daniel had almost opened his practice with a partner years before, but the two had argued on its basic setup. The other doctor wanted to run the practice as a private business while Daniel was adamant on operating as a nonprofit. Daniel won, but it cost him his partner in the process. Still, seeing how he was able to help his patients at a reasonable rate was reason enough for him every day.

"I see," said Amanda. She picked up her pen and pretended to write. "Unable to cooperate with those around him."

"Hey!" laughed Daniel.

Amanda grinned. "Just kidding."

Daniel was caught by the sight of her smile. Last night she'd been adorably disheveled from her long trip, but today she was every bit the polished businesswoman with no chink in her armor. But when she smiled, he thought he saw that image slip a little, enough for a glimpse of the real woman underneath to show through. A woman that he wouldn't mind becoming friends with, if circumstances were different. He'd have to keep reminding himself that she was here on business. She held his professional fate in her hands.

Luckily, Amanda didn't seem to pick up on any of the thoughts running through his head. She was busy making notes. "So once the clinic is finished, how do you plan on meeting the increased number of patients? Do you have other doctors who are planning to join in?"

Daniel frowned. He knew that this was the weakest point of his otherwise strong plan. "In the beginning, I expect it will be just me." Amanda's eyebrows rose, but he continued. "The issue is that we don't have many doctors in town, and my colleagues are already overwhelmed with caseloads of their own. A few of them may take advantage of the new center, but, from my conversations with them, none are willing or able to take on a larger role. I am hopeful that, over time, the excellent facilities will attract some doctors who might be willing to work here fulltime. They will likely require some additional training, of course. I'm sure you remember that there's not a ton of training in medical school that is tailored to a rural practice."

"No, I suppose not. You have to be prepared for a wider variety of cases in the country. Patients don't have access to as many specialists as you would in an urban setting."

"Exactly," said Daniel, pleased with her grasp on the challenges. "But it's nothing that can't be fixed with on-the-ground experience. Once the center is actually built, I think the doctor staffing issues will be sorted out with time."

He hoped.

"We'll stick a pin in that for the moment," said Amanda. "I'd like to go over the budget with you again, if you don't mind."

"Sure," said Daniel, leaning forward and rummaging across the desk. "I've got copies right here." He found the correct papers and pulled them out of a pile of medical charts, bumping the picture frame that he kept on his desk.

Amanda accepted her copy from Daniel and then reached out to straighten the picture frame. She paused with her hand on the picture.

"Oh my goodness, these boys are adorable," she said. "Are they your sons?" Was it his imagination, or did she hesitate slightly before asking the question?

"No," Daniel said, "they're my nephews. I'm not married." He cringed. Had he just said that out loud? It sounded like he was hitting on her. He hurried to move on.

Tilting the picture frame so he could see too, he continued talking. "This one is Robert, and this is Ethan. They're my brother's boys. Just a little over a year old." He couldn't keep the affection out of his voice as he talked about them. He'd be the first to admit that Robert and Ethan were two of the brightest spots in his life.

Daniel studied Amanda carefully as she looked at the picture, wondering if she would comment on what was the obvious difference between the twins. It was there for all to see, even as babies.

Robert was your typical, active one-year-old. He was constantly on the move, into everything, driving his sister-in-law, Sarah, to distraction with his ability to make trouble and keep up a steady stream of chatter, some nonsense, some not, while he was doing it.

Ethan was very different. He still chose to sit over his newfound ability to walk. He had just begun to babble, to his parents' delight, but he wasn't forming many recognizable words yet. He enjoyed watching Robert explore and tear up the house, but never joined in himself.

Daniel vividly remembered the day that Sarah had gone in for her twenty-week ultrasound and first found out that one of the twins likely had Down syndrome. Sarah and Kyle, his brother, had a late afternoon appointment. He'd made them promise to swing by his practice when they were done to tell him the big gender reveal.

He knew something was off when they came in to his office. Sarah and Kyle didn't look as happy as he'd expected. The doctor in him immediately started worrying, mentally ticking off all the bad news items that they could have received.

"Well?" he asked, trying to ignore his misgivings and be cheerful. "What's the verdict?"

Kyle glanced at Sarah, sliding his arm along her back, and turned back to Daniel with a smile. "Good news for us. We're getting two boys."

"Two boys!" Daniel stood and pumped his fist. "I knew it. Men for the win!" He shook his head teasingly. "Poor Sarah, you're going to be so outnumbered."

"I am," said Sarah, who looked somewhat dazed. She took a deep breath. "We also got some more news."

As they proceeded to give Daniel the rundown of what their obstetrician said, he had mixed feelings. He knew they'd been thrown for a loop, but he also realized how many worse outcomes there could have been to that day. He was prepared to give them a pep talk, to help them see how they could manage Down syndrome, and even reap some unexpected blessings from it, when he found that they didn't need a pep talk at all.

"So, we're a little bit in shock, I guess," Kyle finished up.

Sarah looked at him and seemed to finally shake some of the dazed expression. "No," she said calmly. "Not anymore." She smiled and stole her hand into Kyle's. "We've got two healthy babies. That's what matters."

Kyle took a deep breath and locked eyes with Sarah. "Right. Two healthy babies."

Daniel walked around his desk to hug them both. "Two healthy babies," he echoed as he wrapped his arms around their shoulders. "Two healthy *boy* babies."

When he heard Sarah laugh, he knew they'd be fine.

When Kyle and Sarah left though, he looked around his office. He thought of his small pediatric practice, the shortage of doctors in town, and the outsized needs that children with Down syndrome could have. He thoughts of the lengthy drive to get to a medical center with the sort of resources that Kyle and Sarah would need. And then and there, he hatched a plan.

All of which brought him to this present moment with Amanda, the woman who could make that plan a reality. She was still looking at the picture of the boys.

"They're beautiful," she said. "Both of them."

Daniel watched as she restored the picture frame to its usual place.

"I bet they keep their parents running nonstop," she added.

Daniel nodded, noting that she'd made no mention of Ethan's syndrome although surely she must have noticed. "Kyle and Sarah," he said, feeling that he wanted Amanda to know his family's names. "That's my brother and sister-in-law." He swallowed. "And yes, they're always in a state of barely controlled chaos."

"Kyle and Sarah," she repeated with a smile. She cocked her head sideways and looked as if she were waiting for something. Finally, she asked gently, "So, the budget?"

Daniel shook his head clear. "Right."

He was going to have to watch himself, he thought as he pulled out the correct papers. He had business to conduct. It wouldn't do to get too attached to Amanda.

AS WAS his usual custom, Daniel stayed late that evening. He had a list of follow-up questions spread before him, courtesy of Amanda. His homework – he laughed to himself thinking how she'd called it that – was to work through the questions so that they could discuss it in the morning.

He read the next on the list. "How would you characterize the demand for an expanded facility in your community?" He rocked back in his chair and thought of the parade of patients who came through his door. He had at least two patients who needed dedicated physical therapists, and three were going to have to travel within the next six months to get tubes in their ears. One more case of strep throat for Tyler Wiggins would mean his tonsils had to come out, which required another out-of-town surgical trip. And even though Rita Mulvaney had made great strides in speaking over the last several months, she really needed to see a trained speech pathologist. And these were only his cases alone; there were bound to be more from other doctors in the area. He leaned back over his desk and began typing.

"Knock, knock."

Daniel looked up to see his brother Kyle standing in the door. In many ways, Kyle looked like the complete opposite of Daniel. He was short and stocky, and he kept his sandy hair buzzed short. But they shared the same golden brown eyes and propensity to grin.

"Where'd you come from? I didn't even hear the door."

Kyle slid into Daniel's visitor chair. "Hard at work, bro?"

"Yep. I've had a rep here from the Weisman Trust all day. She's putting me through my paces."

"Hey, that's great! How's it going so far?"

Daniel frowned. "I think it's going well. She's slightly hard to read, but it seems like she likes the clinic. And she's asked some tricky questions, but nothing I couldn't answer." He ran his fingers through his hair, inexplicably finding himself thinking about the rare glimpses of humor he'd caught from her throughout the day. "She seems friendly. I just wish I could know for sure if she's going to recommend us for the grant or not."

"You're doing the best you can. No need to stress about it more."

Daniel shook his head. "Easier said than done."

"Well you know what I'd say to that," said Kyle. "You just gotta give it to God. Take some of the weight off your shoulders and put it where it belongs."

Daniel inwardly rolled his eyes. Trust in his brother to downplay all the hard work it had taken to get to this point, and how much hard work was still to come. Just give it to God, and everything will be ok. He wished it were that easy.

"Speaking of taking a weight off," said Kyle, "Sarah sent me to bring you home for dinner. She said you're working too hard."

"She did, huh?"

"You know, Sarah."

Daniel sighed. "Thanks, Kyle. And give my thanks to your wife. But I really can't. I've got a mountain of work to get through before tomorrow. I want to be ready for Amanda."

"Amanda?" asked Kyle.

"The grant officer. Dr. Garvas."

"You called her Amanda."

"She asked me to."

"Interesting…" said Kyle, drawing the word out.

Daniel snorted. "What does that mean?"

Kyle raised his hands in surrender. "Nothing at all. Forget I said anything." He dropped his hands. "So, if she's a doctor, what's she doing working for a Trust giving out money?"

Daniel leaned back. "You know, I was wondering that, too. I mean, who goes through all the studying and pain and expense of medical school only to give it up?" He shook his head. "I couldn't do it. I'd miss my patients way too much."

"Maybe she feels like she can do more good this way," said Kyle. "I mean, she's not helping patients directly anymore, but she can certainly help a lot of patients down the road by opening the new medical center."

"Maybe."

"And who knows how many grants she's helped get approved?" continued Kyle. "You're probably just one of several big projects she's got going on. She could be helping thousands of patients through various people."

"Geez, why don't you go work for the Trust?" asked Daniel. "You're a great evangelizer for it." He didn't know why, but the thought of being just one of Amanda's many projects irked him.

"I'm only saying, there's more than one way to serve patients, just like there's more than one way to serve God." He stood to go. "Sarah's going to be disappointed. You sure you won't come? You can get in some quality baby/uncle bonding time. Don't want to the boys to forget what you look like."

"It's because of the boys that I've got to stay, Kyle. You know that."

Kyle clapped him on the shoulder. "You're a good guy, Daniel. Terrible at accepting dinner invitations. But a good guy." He started to leave, but paused in the doorway and turned back.

"This Amanda…"

"Yeah?"

"She an older lady? Grey hair. Experienced? That sort of thing?"

Daniel shook his head. "No, she's young, but she obviously knows what she's doing."

"Ah, ok… She's probably not especially attractive, is she?"

Daniel felt unaccountably annoyed. "I don't see what it has to do with anything, but she happens to be beautiful. Not that it matters."

"Right. Doesn't matter." Kyle waved his hands dismissively. "Anyways, have a good day tomorrow. With *Amanda*."

Daniel just stopped himself from throwing a book at his brother's head on his way out. After all, he thought, why damage a perfectly good book? He wasn't overly concerned about his brother's head.

He ignored Kyle's laughter coming from down the hall and got back to work.

AMANDA COULDN'T relax that evening. She bounced around her hotel room, unable to settle to anything. She tried working on her grantee report but couldn't concentrate. Her room TV couldn't hold her interest. The books she brought for bedtime reading seemed dull. Finally, she pulled a light jacket over her pink flannel pajamas and headed out for an evening walk.

Once outside, the moonlight provided enough light to see her way. Most of the buildings were dark, including Daniel's office. She supposed people must go to sleep early in the little town.

Up ahead, she saw the swing on the pediatrician's porch sway in a light breeze. It was like it was calling to her, inviting her to come rest for a while.

She couldn't resist.

She settled back onto the swing, enjoying the gentle rocking motion. It gave a slight creak each time she swung backward, the rhythm soothing her unsettled nerves. She leaned her head back and was just starting to relax when she was startled to herself again. The front door of the doctor's office had opened.

She saw Daniel pull the door shut behind him and lock the door. Amanda froze. She knew she should say something and alert him to her presence, but she couldn't find any words.

Daniel turned to go down the steps, but pulled up short when he saw Amanda sitting there.

"Oh," he said in surprise.

Well, this is awkward, she thought. She gave a small wave and what she hoped was an apologetic smile.

"I'm so sorry," she said, standing up. "I didn't realize anyone was here. The building was all dark."

"That's my fault," said Daniel. "I was working back in my office. You can't see the light from out front." He paused. "Is everything ok?"

"Yes, it's fine. I just wanted to go for a quick walk before bed, and your porch swing was kind of calling to me."

Before bed… Oh no! She glanced down at her clothes before she could stop herself. She was in her pajamas! She groaned inwardly and snapped her head back up, hoping that he hadn't noticed.

Daniel smiled. "I'm a sucker for a good swing, myself." He gestured back to the swing. "Don't let me stop you."

Amanda sat back down, sure that she must look ridiculous. "Thanks."

Daniel leaned against the nearest post. "You seem tired."

Amanda laughed self-consciously. "Just what every woman wants to hear."

"No, I meant –"

"Don't worry about it," she said. "You're right. I am tired. It's been a while since I was on my feet all day, in and out of patients' rooms."

"Not much rest in doing the rounds, is there?"

"Nope."

There was a pause in the conversation before Daniel spoke. "If you don't mind my asking, why aren't you in medicine anymore?"

"I am in medicine," she said quickly. "Seventy-five percent of the grants that come through the Trust are in healthcare, so my medical knowledge comes in handy all the time." She sat up. "Just the other day I reviewed a request for funding for medical research that could help treat childhood diabetes. My medical training was very helpful there in understanding the proposal."

"Sure," said Daniel. "I can see that. I'm sorry. I didn't mean to assume anything."

She sensed that he was trying to defuse the situation. Her shoulders relaxed. "It's fine. I'm guess I'm a little touchy." She looked up at him. "I admit, I'm maybe not quite as active in medicine as I used to be." She paused. "I was trained as a pulmonologist. I spent the first five years after I finished my residency in a practice a lot like yours, treating allergies and asthma, things like that." She poked a toe out at a piece of playground equipment near her. "Well, maybe the office wasn't exactly like yours." She smiled. "We didn't have a playground in our waiting room."

"Hey, I'll have you know that the playground is a big hit with my patient population."

"Oh, I know." She grinned. "I saw that 'patient population' having a great time out here all day." She sighed and leaned her head back. "Truthfully, today was a pretty fun day. It was a nice change."

"Maybe you should join me."

She was startled. "What?" She searched his face, trying to gauge if he was serious. Was it her imagination, or did Daniel look embarrassed for a moment?

The moment was gone quickly, however, and Daniel answered her in a joking tone that put her back at ease. "Yeah, maybe while you're here checking me out, you could help treat some patients. Nothing shows you how a doctor operates like working with him. And I could get some cheap labor."

Amanda laughed. "Yes, I'm sure that would work out great for you. Everyone wants to go to a doctor with rusty skills."

"It's like riding a bike. What could go wrong?"

"Plenty," she said, troubled by the thoughts his words had evoked. "Plenty," she repeated almost to herself.

She noticed him watching her with curiosity, and maybe even concern. Time to act like the professional that she was.

So she stood and said as brightly as she could manage, "Thanks for the loan of the porch swing. I think I'm ready to turn in for the night."

Daniel stepped back to let her pass down the steps. "Come by anytime. I promise not to interrupt you either."

"Don't be silly," she said. "It's your porch. And it was nice." She smiled. "See you in the morning."

"I'll be here."

With a quick wave, Amanda descended the steps and walked down the street toward the hotel.

DANIEL WATCHED her go, admiring her light form as she skipped back across the street.

That was a close one. He didn't know what he'd been thinking, blurting out that she should join him in the practice. Luckily, he'd been able to turn it to a joke, but for just a minute, he knew that he'd spoken seriously. He told himself that he'd been momentarily distracted, caught up by the sight of a pajama-clad Amanda relaxing on his porch swing, almost as if she were meant to be there. But another part of him seemed to recognize some hazy truth that had come unbidden into his mind – that here was someone who could be a good partner.

Professionally, of course, he added inwardly.

But Daniel knew couldn't go inviting people to join his practice on a whim after one day's acquaintance. Amanda would think he was insane, and he needed to appear like the calm, rational doctor that he was if he was going to get this grant. Besides, he couldn't help feeling there was something Amanda was not telling him. It was too soon in their acquaintance for him to ask for more information, but he was definitely curious.

All he wanted was to open a new clinic, but he had the feeling that he'd gotten himself into something much bigger than that.

CHAPTER 3

The next morning found Amanda deep in consultation with Daniel about the new center's building plans. She was trying to be as professional as possible, with last night's memory of the unexpected meeting on her mind.

I can't believe I was in my PJs, she thought yet again. *How embarrassing.*

She was seated at Daniel's desk surrounded by paperwork. She looked over the report he'd compiled on construction details, trying to focus her mind on the grant and not on her embarrassment from the night before.

She switched papers. "You really expect to be able to build the facility using local labor?" she asked.

"Partially," he said. He stood in the corner of the room, bouncing a racquetball, first against the floor then the wall before catching it smoothly back in his hand. He'd said it helped him to think. "I know we'll definitely have to use some outside help," he continued, "but as you can see in the attached bid, I've reached an agreement with the construction company that they will hire at least 30% of their workers from here in the community."

Very impressive, thought Amanda as she flipped through the bid paperwork. Her Type-A detail-oriented brain could appreciate the work that had gone into Daniel's proposal. She absentmindedly began tapping her toes in rhythm with the ball. "And do you think the local economy can provide that amount of labor?"

He grinned. "So Ernie tells me."

"Ernie?"

"Ernie Christie. He's our local ranching expert. A bunch of the work around here is cyclical in nature, and a project like this could be a Godsend to people who are looking for more work in the down season without having to leave town."

Amanda tapped her pen against her cheek. "In that case, we'd better go over these construction timelines. I've got a couple questions –" She was interrupted by a knock on the door. One of the nurses poked her head in.

"Sorry, Dr. Shane." She had a smile on her face. "You have a visitor." She stepped back and ushered in a small girl of three or four before slipping back out the door.

The child had bright red, curly hair and a mat of light brown freckles across her nose and cheeks. She looked shyly around the room, but lit up as soon as her eyes found Daniel. Amanda was just thinking that she looked familiar when the girl was followed into the room by Millie, the waitress from the diner. She carried a large, square canvas bag with rigid sides, and her eyes widened when she spotted Amanda in the room.

"I'm so sorry to interrupt, Doctor," Mille said. "I didn't know you had company." She looked distinctly interested in Amanda's presence.

"Hi, Millie," said Daniel. "This is Dr. Amanda Garvas. She's visiting from the Weisman Trust." He turned to Amanda.

"We've met," said Millie with a grin at Amanda, "but it's nice to see you again."

Meanwhile, Daniel was greeting the little girl. "And how are you, Miss Rita?"

Rita smiled. "Good." Her expression turned suddenly serious. "But we've got a cat problem," she said with a heavy lisp.

"Oh, dear," said Daniel, matching her concerned tone. "Why don't you tell me what it's all about?"

Millie took over. "I really wasn't sure where we should go, and you seemed like the best bet. I was cleaning up the breakfast rush at the diner, when my babysitter called me. You see, this cat showed up at our house, and we're fairly sure she's having kittens. I mean, she's enormous and very grouchy, and she keeps straining pretty hard. But I really know nothing about cat labor. I mean, I know nothing about cats, I obviously don't know what their labor is supposed to be like, and I'm worried something might be wrong, so I thought I'd better bring her along for you to look at." She gestured to the bag she was carrying. "She's in here. I made her as comfortable as possible, but who can be comfy during labor, am I right?"

As she continued to speak, she carefully set the bag on the desk on top of the mishmash of papers so that everyone could peer in.

Amanda looked in and saw a beautiful tabby in obvious distress. As she watched, she could see a contraction take hold as the animal's stomach clenched and contorted. Her eyes rose and met Daniel's. The cat was definitely in labor.

Rita had waited silently while her mother told the story, but now she gently put her hand on Daniel's arm and spoke. "Dr. Shane," she said, "can you help?"

Daniel put his hand over hers. "Of course I can." He grinned and then rubbed his hands together. "Ok, we'll start by getting this little mama out of her cocoon so she can move around if she wants to. Dr. Garvas, perhaps you'll assist?"

He reached in to carefully lift the cat while Amanda held the top of the bag as wide open as possible. The cat gave one indignant meow but otherwise submitted to the help.

"Better shut the door," instructed Daniel, "so she doesn't bolt." Millie ran to pull the door closed as Daniel lowered the animal. Once the cat's feet hit the floor, she began pacing back and forth from the desk to the door.

Amanda stared at the cat, completely at a loss of how to proceed. Luckily, Daniel seemed much more competent in this area. He turned to Millie. "Any idea how long she's been in active labor. I mean, actually pushing and straining?"

Millie shook her head. "At least an hour, but that's about all I can say for sure. We don't even know where she came from."

"Poor kitty," murmured Rita so quietly Amanda almost didn't hear.

Daniel ran his hands through his hair, a gesture that Amanda had learned to mean that he was thinking. "The good news," he said, "is that most cats get through labor just fine without any help from people, and one hour is fairly normal for the feline active labor stage. The bad news is that it could have been going on longer than we know, which could indicate that something's amiss." He turned to Millie and gave her a meaningful look. "Maybe it would be best for you to take Miss Rita to play on the front porch for a little bit."

Millie nodded and grabbed Rita's hand. "Ok, sweetie, let's go play on the slides."

"But I don't want to leave."

Daniel squatted down by Rita and looked into her eyes. "You go have fun while we take care of this, ok?" He spoke calmly and cheerfully, and Amanda could appreciate the effects of a good bedside manner. "When you come back, we might have some new kittens for you to meet!"

Rita reluctantly allowed her mother to lead her from the room, throwing pitiful looks back over her shoulder at the cat as she went.

"Millie," Amanda called as they left, "would you please ask the nurse to bring back some old towels or something?" They couldn't very well have the cat give birth on patient files.

"Good idea," said Daniel. "We've got some spare linens in the supply closet. They'll know where they are."

"Will do," said Millie. She whisked Rita from the room, pausing only to mouth a quick "thank you" to the two doctors on the way out.

As soon as she'd left the room, Amanda turned to face Daniel. "How on earth do you know the normal length of active labor for a cat?"

He laughed. "What? Don't you?"

"And why did they bring the cat to you? I mean, I'm glad they trust you, but why aren't they going to a vet?"

"I'm sure our vets are busy with animals that are a little more commercially important," he said simply. "They keep pretty busy this time of year with the farmers and ranchers. A homeless tabby cat is unlikely to be high on the priority list. Believe it or not, this is not the first cat birth I've attended." One corner of his mouth turned up. "As we discussed, rural doctors have to be ready for anything."

Amanda shook her head. "Forget about your new clinic. You guys should apply for a grant to bring a few more veterinarians to town. Think how much time it'd clear up if you weren't taking care of the animals." She rubbed her forehead as she watched Daniel walk to a set of cabinets behind his desk, from which he removed a box of rubber gloves.

"Ok, what are you doing?" she demanded.

"You know what I'm doing. Prepping in case I need to deliver me some kittens." He pulled out a set for himself before tossing the box to her. "Care to assist?"

Amanda stared at him. She could just imagine herself asking for the promotion at work when she got back to Seattle and listing feline midwifery as one of her new skills. *I cannot believe I'm doing this*, she thought.

Forty minutes later, the exhausted tabby lay in a pile of blankets with four, hungry kittens blindly pushing to her side for milk.

In the end, the cat had only needed a little intervention. The first kitten was barely stuck, but Daniel was able to get her quickly free. Afterwards, Amanda and Daniel were free to sit back and let nature take care of the rest.

Amanda had assisted in the birth of several babies during her residency and had even delivered a few children single handedly. There was nothing to match that feeling of bringing a new life into the world, that first glimpse of the truly unconditional love that God blesses all parents with, and watching the tabby fearlessly push out her kittens brought back fond memories of the babies Amanda had delivered.

She looked over at Daniel, and they shared a quiet smile. She had to admit, as a young resident, she could never have pictured herself ending up here – a non-practicing doctor assisting in a cat birth. But something about it had been so satisfying. And she had to admire the presence of mind Daniel showed to save the first kitten.

Once the newborns were settled and happily nursing, Amanda went herself to fetch Millie and Rita from the play area. She stuck her head out of the front door and spotted Rita.

"Ready to come meet some kittens?" she called.

Rita squealed and rushed past her, and Millie wasn't far behind. Amanda laughed and followed them back.

She found Rita staring rapturously at the kittens, her small hands clasped in front of her so tightly that Amanda could see her knuckles turning white.

"I think she likes them," Amanda said quietly to Millie as she watched the little girl. "I hate to tell you this, but I think you might have a cat now." When Millie didn't answer, Amanda turned to look at her, where she was met with almost the identical star-struck attitude, right down to the white knuckles. Like mother, like daughter, she thought in amusement.

Amanda looked up and caught Daniel's eye, and she felt the connection of a silent, shared laugh.

If only practicing medicine could always be so pleasant.

GIVEN THE unexpected events of the morning, the rest of the day was rushed. Amanda shadowed Daniel with his patients, whose appointments were all a little behind schedule thanks to the kittens' arrivals. Somehow every child had heard the news and wanted to see the new babies. Daniel had to repeatedly explain that the kittens had gone home with their mother, but he showed everyone who asked pictures of the sweet animals that he'd taken with his phone. Amanda marveled at his patience as he went through the same discussion and showed the same photos twenty times.

Because of the patient backlog, Amanda didn't have the chance to finish going over the grant questions that she'd assigned to Daniel, so it had to be pushed off to the next day. Normally, she'd chafe at the delay in her schedule, but somehow she didn't seem to mind. She still had a few days in town; she'd manage to fit it all in.

She was pleased with how the grant was going. After her observations, she felt sure that Daniel was professionally very competent. The two of them still needed to work out some details of the actual project, but that would come with time.

Yes, on the whole, she was feeling pretty good about things when she said goodnight to Daniel and left the office for the night.

She'd already decided to go back to the diner for her evening meal, hoping to check in with Millie on how the kittens were doing.

When she pushed open the doors, the restaurant was already hopping with the dinner crowd. It was noisy with chatter and the occasional yell or squeal from little kids, and waitresses ran back and forth. Sliding into a free seat at the bar, Amanda reflected that she'd seen more cowboys in these few days in Highland Canyon than she had in a lifetime in Seattle.

She pulled open a menu but immediately shut it again. Who was she kidding? She knew she was getting that scrumptious pot roast again.

Amanda saw Millie floating from table to table as she greeted customers and filled water glasses. When Millie spotted her, she cried out, "Amanda!" and made a beeline towards her. Amanda ducked her head, embarrassed. Millie had yelled loud enough for the whole restaurant to notice, and now a sort of hush had fallen over the room.

When Millie reached her side, she threw an arm around her shoulders.

"Everyone," Millie continued, "if you haven't met her yet, this is Dr. Amanda Garvas, and she helped Dr. Shane today to deliver all of Ella's kittens!"

The room broke into polite applause, and Amanda gave a small wave before turning around in her seat. She knew that her cheeks must be on fire.

"You named the cat 'Ella?'" she asked once Millie let her go.

"Rita picked it. She's very into Cinderella right now."

"So the cat's staying, huh? How about all those kittens?"

"Sure thing. We haven't gotten around to naming all of them yet, though. We'll have to keep tabs on their personalities." She paused. "You know, when my husband died, I considered getting a cat and becoming a crazy cat lady." She laughed. "I guess God thought I needed to get on with it and sent me five cats to start me on my way."

Amanda's mouth fell open. "Oh, Millie, I'm so sorry. I didn't realize you were a widow."

Millie patted her arm. "Don't apologize. It was years ago, right after Rita was born. I'm able to talk about it now. I can smile about him instead of cry. Now, what do you want to eat? It's on the house."

"No, it's not," said Amanda.

"Yes, it is. You delivered those sweet kittens, who by the way seem to be doing great, and you made my daughter the happiest I've ever seen her outside of Christmas morning. It's my pleasure."

"Really, you shouldn't. Daniel did what little work there was to be done."

Millie raised her eyebrows. "Daniel, hmm?"

"Yes. I mean, Dr. Shane. Whatever." Amanda felt heat rising up her neck.

"Uh huh," said Millie with a knowing grin. "Dr. Shane will be getting his free dinner, too, don't you worry, except he always orders his to be delivered to his office. He's got a bad habit of working late. So since you're here, you're going to have to take the full brunt of my gratitude."

"Um..." Amanda wondered how to say the next sentence delicately. "Are you allowed to give out free meals?"

Millie looked momentarily confused. Then her expression cleared, and she gave out a high peal of laughter.

"What'd I say?" asked Amanda uncertainly.

"Sorry," said Millie, still giggling. "I just figured out what you meant. I'm not a waitress here. This is my restaurant. I'm the owner."

Amanda's mouth dropped open. "I'm so sorry! Again! I didn't realize you owned the diner."

"No big deal," said Millie, still laughing. "But as you can see, it'll probably be ok with my boss if I give you a free meal. Seeing's as how I am the boss."

Even Amanda had to laugh. "Well, ok," she said. "If you're going to completely twist my arm –"

"I am."

"Then I'd better have the pot roast. And thank you."

"Coming right up!" said Millie as she whisked away again.

Amanda took a sip of the water glass that Millie had unobtrusively left behind. It really had been a fun day. She thought of Daniel's joke the night before that she stay behind and help in his practice for a while. She knew he'd been kidding, but did a tiny part of her think it wouldn't be so bad?

Solely because of the interesting work, she told herself, not because of Daniel.

Just then an elderly man sat down in the seat next to her. He wore a tan cowboy hat and mud-spattered clothing. He gave her a wordless nod before he turned to his menu.

When Millie swung back by a few minutes later, she greeted the older cowboy.

"Hi, Ern!" she said. "Glad you see you're back in town. Everything go ok out there?"

He nodded and gave a simple, "Yep." His voice was low and gravelly.

Amanda was starting to suspect that he was a man of few words. A memory stirred within her of an earlier conversation with Daniel. Hadn't he mentioned a rancher named Ernie? Ernie Christie?"

Amanda spoke tentatively. "Mr. Christie?"

He turned to her and raised a set of bushy eyebrows. "Yes'm?"

"I'm working with Dr. Shane," she said. "He mentioned you were the local ranching expert."

"That's Ernie, all right," said Millie.

Ernie looked at Amanda stoically. Finally, he said, "Dr. Shane's a good man."

Amanda hesitated to answer, wondering whether there was more information coming. But the rancher seemed content with his statement and went back to the menu.

Millie looked at Amanda with a twinkle in her eye. "He really is," she said. "Ernie's lack of description, notwithstanding. I adore him. He has done more for my daughter than I thought was possible."

"That's right," said Amanda, remembering Millie's comments from her first night in town. She leaned forward, ready to gather information for her report. "I'd love to hear more, if you don't mind."

"Of course I don't mind. This is what happened. Now Rita had always been behind on speaking. Oh, she talked a lot but she never really started picking up real words from us. It was always gibberish. Anyway, we couldn't really figure out the reason why. Finally, when Rita was three and still not speaking clearly, our regular doctor finally referred us to Dr. Shane for a second opinion, and it took him one appointment – only one – to diagnose the problem. Rita couldn't hear! Well," Millie cocked her head sideways, "she could technically hear, which was why our old doc never caught it, but the words were all garbled to her. And if that's what you hear, that's what you'll learn to speak, right?"

It made sense to Amanda. "Sure."

"So, Dr. Shane did surgery on her to correct her ears – we had to drive three full hours to the nearest surgical center, mind you – and then afterward he has tirelessly worked with Rita every step of the way. Her language skills have come so far since then."

"That's wonderful," said Amanda. "So you'd give him good marks in patient satisfaction?"

"Good marks? Try amazing marks. Stupendous marks. Whatever's the highest."

"Noted," said Amanda. "Stupendous marks. I hope all his patients are as enthused as you are."

"They are," said Millie. "Just ask around, and you'll see." She looked toward a corner booth. "Uh oh, I see a spill. I'd better go take care of that!"

As Millie bustled off, Amanda felt someone tap her on the shoulder. She swiveled in her chair to see a tall, blond woman with kind blue eyes.

"Hi," she said. "I hope you don't think I'm overstepping, but I heard Millie introduce you. You're the doctor in town from the Weisman Trust, right? The one working with Dr. Shane's office?"

"Yes, that's me," said Amanda.

The woman smiled. "I thought I recognized your name. I'm Sarah Shane, Daniel's sister-in-law." She pointed over her shoulder to where a stocky man was seated at a round table with two babies in highchairs. "That's Daniel's brother, Kyle, with our boys."

Seeing the two women looking at him, the man gave a small wave. Amanda thought he looked a little sheepish, which made her wonder whose idea it had been for Sarah to come introduce herself.

"It's very nice to meet you," said Amanda.

"If you're not here with anyone," Sarah went on, "why don't you come sit with us? We'd love to hear more about the work you do and how it's going with Daniel."

"Oh, no, I don't want to impose."

"Please, we'd love it," said Sarah in such a gentle voice that Amanda immediately believed her. She smiled her assent and grabbed her water glass.

"See you later, Mr. Christie," said Amanda, and her seatmate nodded in reply.

Amanda turned to Sarah. "Lead the way."

At the table, Sarah introduced her husband, and Amanda was struck by the similarity in his eyes to Daniel's. But that thought only made her wonder when exactly she'd noticed Daniel's eyes, so she quickly pushed it away.

"Please to meet you, Amanda," said Kyle. "I've heard nice things about you from Daniel."

"Thanks," said Amanda, feeling unaccountably pleased.

Next, Sarah showed Amanda their two twin boys, and the love and pride was so obvious in her voice that it turned Amanda's thoughts from Daniel completely.

"This is Robert," said Sarah, tickling the baby closest to Kyle.

"Mama," he said clearly, pointing to Sarah.

Sarah laughed. "He introduces me to everyone he meets." She turned to the other baby and softly rubbed his head. He gave her a toothy grin in reward. "And this is Ethan."

Amanda took the empty seat held out for her by Kyle and then turned back to the babies. "Hi, guys," she said, as she reached out and gave them both a hand to hold. Robert took hold enthusiastically and started pulling on her arm. Ethan was more cautious. He stroked the back of her hand with his finger before finally grabbing on.

Amanda was absolutely entranced. "You two are adorable. Every sweet thing your uncle said about you is absolutely true, isn't it? I bet you never give your parents any trouble, do you?"

Ethan picked that moment to pull her hand to his mouth and start drooling on it.

"Oh, I'm so sorry," said Sarah, handing her a napkin. "I think he's teething."

"Don't worry about it," said Amanda. She let the napkin sit on the table in front of her, rather than interrupt

Ethan in his explorations. "I've been in contact with many grosser things than baby spit in my time."

"You sound like Daniel," said Kyle. "It's impossible to gross him out."

"And these two have tried," said Sarah, gesturing to the babies. "You should see Daniel when he babysits. He always comes out of it covered in spit-up."

"Or worse," laughed Kyle.

"Daniel babysits?" Amanda asked.

"Of course I babysit," said a voice behind her.

DANIEL COULDN'T quite describe the feelings he'd gone through upon entering the diner and finding Amanda playing with his nephews. Something about the scene felt so right.

When he spoke, Amanda jumped in surprise, pulling her hands out of the babies' grasps. He was sorry to have startled her and ruined the adorable scene.

Daniel ignored the looks of surprise on Kyle's and Sarah's faces. He could come in and eat dinner if he wanted to. No need to act like they had just seen the risen Lord.

Kyle stood up and walked to clap his brother on the back. "Daniel! I can't believe you stopped working long enough to eat."

"Don't be so dramatic," said Daniel, grabbing the last empty chair at the table. "I eat every night."

"Yeah, huddled at that desk of yours."

"Leave him alone, Kyle," murmured Sarah, but Daniel could see that she was holding back a smile. True, it was possible that he'd seen Amanda from his office go into the diner. And maybe that had something to do with his coming in tonight. But he didn't have to acknowledge that to them.

Daniel turned and greeted his nephews. They were always happy to see him. Robert was clamoring to leave his highchair in favor of Uncle Daniel's lap. He lifted his arms up expectantly to Daniel.

"Do you mind?" he asked Sarah.

"Go for it, but you have to get him back in when dinner comes."

Daniel pulled Robert into his arms and together they started playing peek-a-boo with Ethan. He noticed Amanda watching them with an amused expression on her face.

"So, Amanda," Daniel asked as he covered his eyes with Robert's hands, "have you recovered from our veterinary adventure today?"

"I have," she replied, "and I even got a free dinner out of it. Once Millie gets a load of you, I'm sure you will, too."

"It's my lucky day," he said. "Free help at the office and free food." He removed the hands from his eyes and leaned over to Robert. "Peek-a-boo!" Robert gurgled in response.

"How is the project going?" asked Sarah. "Forgive me, but I don't really know what kind of work is entailed in applying for a grant like this."

"It's going well," said Amanda. "Basically, we're going over the details of the proposal, including how the clinic would be built and how it would be operated. And I'm taking extra time to get a feel for how Daniel's practice runs now so that I can tell our Board about the key personnel who will be involved in the project."

"She's checking me out," clarified Daniel, "to make sure I know what I'm doing."

"That's a little bit of an oversimplification," said Amanda.

"But it's basically it."

"Well… kind of," Amanda admitted.

"So, what's the verdict?" asked Kyle. "Is Daniel up to snuff?"

Daniel locked eyes with Amanda. He raised his eyebrows questioningly and enjoyed watching a slight blush spread across her face.

"The jury's still out," she said.

BACK IN her trusty pajamas and cozy socks that evening, Amanda was feeling uncharacteristically optimistic. She didn't know if it was the unorthodox way she'd spent her morning or the pleasant company at dinner, but something had put her into a great mood.

She hummed as she brushed her hair out, remembering the sweet litter of kittens from that morning and then the adorable interactions with Ethan and Robert.

Lots of babies today, she thought. Surely that was responsible for her good mood. Humans were genetically predetermined to love babies. It certainly had nothing to do with the doctor who was with her when those kittens were born or who was so sweet playing peek-a-boo with Ethan and Robert.

She paused in her brushing as she heard her phone ding with a text message. "Any updates?" she read on the screen.

She considered responding to her boss by text, but she knew from experience that would only lead to a text chain a mile long. She might as well call Beth and get it over with.

Beth answered on the first ring. "Ah, Amanda, I was hoping for an update. How goes it?"

"Good," said Amanda. "Better than good. I've got a strong feeling about the project." Amanda went on with her update, and even answering questions from Beth, with half her mind elsewhere. She enjoyed her job and felt that it mattered, but she'd have to admit that sometimes her mind would wander in the middle of these discussions with Beth. Finally, her boss asked a question that snapped her back to reality.

"You working ok with the lead doctor there? What's his name again?"

"Dr. Shane. And, yes, we've got a good workflow going. He's been very accommodating. He's definitely passionate about the new facility." Amanda flopped back onto the bed. "There is a bit of a weak point in that I think he could use some additional manpower, but it isn't insurmountable." Amanda paused and laughed. "He even suggested that I stay on and help for a bit so that he'd get some help around the office. He said I can learn about the practice from the inside out."

Amanda was met with silence.

"Beth? Hello?"

"I'm here," she heard Beth say slowly. "You know, Amanda, that is not the craziest idea I've ever heard. What if you did stay on? Just for a few weeks?"

"Beth," said Amanda. "He was joking. You know, so he could get some free work out of me. Ha ha. It wasn't serious."

"But what if it were? I mean, what if we arranged for you to do that? Because he's not wrong, it would be a great way to really see what makes him tick. What the hidden weaknesses are that we can't discover through a quick grantee investigation visit…"

"Beth –"

"After all, you're still licensed to practice. That's the beauty of the setup. It's one of the main benefits of actually having a doctor working for the Trust. You can be both – doctor and grant officer.

"I really don't think –"

"This could be a trial run. Let's just give it a shot. Because it could revolutionize how we evaluate our grantees. We'd be trendsetters in the industry."

Amanda felt a wave of panic, thinking of years ahead of her dropping into clinics and being a fill-in doctor. She'd moved to the Trust in order to get *away* from medical work. Now she was being pulled right back in!

She sat up on the bed and took a deep breath. Time to try one last attempt. "Beth, I haven't really been asked to do this. He was kidding. I can't insert myself into Dr. Shane's clinic."

"Amanda, you've got to learn one thing. You work for the Weisman Trust now. You absolutely can insert yourself into his practice, into *anyone's* practice, as long as they are asking us for a grant. Do you understand?"

Amanda swallowed. "Yes, Beth. I understand."

"Good. Now don't worry about a thing. I'll call Dr. Shane tomorrow and give him the good news. You should be able to start right away! Let's aim for two to three weeks total, and be sure to take extra good notes. I think we can spare you for that long from the office. I'd really like a detailed report at the end of this, not just to show to the Board of directors regarding this grant, but also to get buy-in for this model of exploring new grants. I really think we're on to something."

Amanda rubbed her hand over her eyes, thankful that her boss couldn't see her right then. When Beth finally hung up the phone a few minutes later, Amanda did the only thing she could think of – she dropped to her knees.

Lord, I don't know what I should do. She dropped her head onto her hands. She knew what she *wanted* to do – run screaming back to Seattle. But presumably that wasn't the best option. She sighed. *Please stay with me and give me the strength to get through this.*

She climbed back into bed and lay back on her pillows. She stared at the ceiling, noticing a small crack that extended from the corner of the room to the ceiling fan gently whirring above her head. She followed that crack across the plaster, feeling like it mirrored the crack that was opening up back inside her.

She didn't want to be a doctor anymore. She'd left that life behind. But it looked like she was getting pulled back in anyway.

CHAPTER 4

Daniel set down the phone at his office desk. *That was interesting.*

His day had begun with an unexpected phone call from Amanda's boss. He'd spoken to Beth a few times on conference calls with Weisman officials, but never one-on-one. Even to his workaholic tendencies she sounded... intense.

But her tone was not the part of the call that preoccupied him now. It was her proposal. She wanted Amanda to stay on at his practice for the next few weeks and help treat patients. And he wasn't sure how he felt about it.

Sure, he knew that it had been his own idea, but it was a suggestion brought on by the temporary madness of a moonlight chat with a beautiful woman. In the cold light of day, he didn't know how well it would work. Amanda hadn't practiced medicine in at least a year, and she wasn't trained as a pediatrician. Was she even qualified to see his patients?

And what about him? He knew enough about himself to know that he liked to be in control when it came to his work. He'd hate to jeopardize the friendship that he felt arising between them because they butted heads over a patient. Or even worse, what if they argued, and he lost her recommendation for the grant? He'd never get the new facility built without the support of the Trust.

Daniel had shared none of these concerns with Beth however. As the potential grantee, he had no power in the situation, and they both knew it. So when Beth outlined her plan, Daniel did the only thing he could do. He said yes.

He pushed himself back from his desk. There was no point in dwelling on it. Short of God sending some sort of miracle escape hatch, this was the situation. He'd just have to do the best he could.

He strode through his office door and down the hallway, greeting nurses as he went. He was surprised that Amanda hadn't arrived yet. The last two days, she'd been the first person in after him.

Then he saw her through the front windows. She was clutching a white paper bag from the diner and a Styrofoam cup of what he guessed was coffee. The bleak expression on her face caught him off guard. No wonder she was late coming in. She looked as though she was absolutely dreading it.

Daniel was surprised. Sure, he had some misgivings about her working there, but this seemed to be something more. He wasn't that bad, was he?

He crossed the waiting room and held open the front door for her.

"Good morning," he said, trying to sound more cheerful than he felt.

She managed a weak smile as she came through the doorway. "Thanks." She held up the paper bag. "Doughnuts, courtesy of Millie. Mama cat and babies all are doing fine." She took a sip of her coffee and closed her eyes.

Daniel took the bag from her. "Awesome. Have you had her doughnuts yet?" He selected a glazed beauty and stuck it in his mouth, holding the open bag out to her.

She eyed the doughnut clenched between his teeth, and he was pleased to see that some of the humor had returned to her face. "No, I haven't, but I guess if they're that tasty." She carefully pulled her doughnut from the bag and took a much smaller bite. "Oh, goodness. That is good."

Daniel rolled the bag shut and grabbed his own doughnut from his mouth, ripping off a bite as he did so. "Now," he said once he'd swallowed, "let's put the rest of these out in the break room and then head to my office. We need to talk."

He tried to ignore how unhappy her nod was as he led the way.

Once in the office, he turned to face her. "I talked to Beth this morning."

She bit her lip, but didn't say anything.

"I take it you've spoken with her, too?" he prompted.

Amanda sighed. "Yes, I have. And I know her crazy idea. And let me start by saying how sorry I am."

"Sorry?" This was not the response that Daniel had expected. "Why?"

"I like working for the Trust, I really do, but sometimes we have a tendency to railroad over our grantees, because they usually will do whatever we want them to." She continued, speaking more quickly now. "And I know that you were only kidding when you asked me to work here, and I told Beth that, but you know Beth – well, I guess you don't – but if you did know Beth you'd know that once she gets an idea in her head, there's no talking her out of it. So now I feel like I'm being forced on you, which you really didn't ask for, and I know you couldn't say no even if you wanted to, which you probably did."

Daniel was silent for a moment before he did something that he couldn't help. He let out a long laugh.

Amanda looked shocked, so Daniel hurried to speak. "I shouldn't laugh, but… no wonder you look so miserable this morning if you're holding all that in!"

"I look miserable?" she asked.

"Completely. But I wish you wouldn't. I admit I was surprised by Beth's idea, but the longer I think about it, the more ok I am with it." Daniel would have been hard-pressed to explain why he suddenly felt so much better about the arrangement. After all, Amanda was only voicing some of the objections that he himself had felt when he first talked to Beth. But he did feel better. Much. Besides, if having Amanda there would help him get the grant, he was all for it. Sharing responsibilities at his office for three weeks was a pretty small price to pay for getting the new clinic.

"If you look at it objectively," he continued, "you're helping me out, so I've got no room at all to complain. I'm getting the extra help of a well qualified doctor."

"You don't know I'm well qualified," said Amanda.

Daniel ignored the fact that he'd had a similar thought not ten minutes before. "Sure, I do."

"You've never seen me practice."

"Then maybe we can tag team patients for the first couple days. I can see you in action. It'll be low pressure."

Daniel thought that his acceptance should have made Amanda feel better, but she looked, if anything, more depressed at this.

"Is there something else you're worried about?" he asked.

Amanda ran her hands over her eyes and sighed. "No," she said finally.

Daniel didn't believe that for one second, but he didn't see how he could force her to confide in him.

Amanda took a sip of her coffee and didn't speak.

Daniel could only watch and wonder what in the world he was supposed to do next.

HALF AN hour later, Daniel paused with his hand on the doorknob to his first consult room. Amanda stood beside him. Her hair was tucked back with a pencil stuck in it, she'd slung Daniel's spare stethoscope around her shoulders, and she was clutching the patient's medical records to her chest in a tight hug. She looked more like a doctor than the businesswoman she typically portrayed, but there was something else in her expression that worried him.

She looked terrified.

"Are you ready?" he asked quietly.

She nodded, but her expression didn't waver. Daniel hesitated to open the door, when she looked up and met his eyes. He felt a quick jolt of electricity. He hadn't realized how close they were standing.

He cleared his throat. "It's just a well-check. Easy peasy."

"Let's go," she said, her voice calmer than he expected.

They stepped into the room, where a young girl of three was sitting on her mother's lap with a book.

"Hello," called Daniel as the mother closed the book and set it aside. "How's everybody doing today?"

The little girl turned and buried her head in her mother's shoulder.

Her mother rolled her eyes good-naturedly. "Good morning, Dr. Shane. We're a little shy this morning."

"That's ok. Georgette, you come out when you're ready." He gestured to Amanda. "I'd like you to meet Dr. Garvas. She's going to be assisting me for the next couple weeks."

"Hi," said the mom with a nod.

Daniel felt rather than heard Amanda take a deep breath, and then she started to conduct the appointment. She sat on the rolling stool Daniel kept in the room and pushed over to the computer. "Let me catch up on your info quickly. Goodness, Georgette, you have been growing!" Georgette's mother beamed and the little girl took a chance on a quick look at Amanda before hiding again.

"You're a full three inches taller now! Someone has been eating her veggies."

Amanda slowly rolled the stool back over to the girl, and Daniel stepped back to give her full room to work.

"Would you like to feel my stethoscope?" she asked quietly. "Actually, it's not mine. It's Dr. Shane's, but he let me borrow it. Do you ever let other kids borrow your toys?"

Georgette slowly lifted her head from her mom to peak at the instrument.

"Actually," Amanda went on in a confiding tone, "this isn't quite what *my* stethoscope looks like. What color is this one?"

"Yellow," said Georgette, apparently forgetting to be shy.

Amanda grinned at the girl. "Very good. You know your colors, don't you?" As she continued talking, she held the instrument against the girl's chest, pausing only to listen to her breathing. "My stethoscope is actually bright green," she said after a moment.

"That's my favorite color," announced Georgette.

"Mine, too!" Amanda slid back. "Your lungs sound great. Can I get a high-five? Good work!"

Daniel watched as Amanda conducted the rest of the appointment. She covered all the necessary steps, was very thorough, and took the time to answer Georgette's mom's questions thoughtfully. With every part of the examination, she managed to put Georgette even more at her ease, so, that by the end of the appointment, the little girl was asking if she could go home and play with Amanda.

Amanda laughed. "She may not feel that way once she gets her shots. The nurse will be here in just a minute to finish up." She leaned down. "Thank you for being such a good patient! When you're done, be sure to get a sticker on your way out, ok?"

"Ok!"

Daniel followed her out of the room, pausing only to give his patient a thumbs-up and remind her mother to call with any questions.

Once in the hallway, he slowly clapped his hands, impressed at the rapport she'd managed to establish so quickly with his patient. "Nicely done, Dr. Garvas. I couldn't have done it better myself."

She turned an attractive shade of pink. "Please, a simple well-check with a sweetheart like that – anybody could have done it."

"Speak for yourself," Daniel said. "The last time Georgette came in, I couldn't get her to talk to me the entire time. Fifteen minutes with you, though, and you're best friends."

Amanda rolled her eyes. "I do not believe you."

Daniel sighed. Clearly she was determined to sell herself short. He wanted to know what was behind this weird reluctance of hers to own her own skills. What had happened in her past to make her so unsure of herself?

She grabbed the chart of the wall of the next room. "Come along, Dr. Shane. We've got lots of patients to see."

This clearly wasn't the time to get to the bottom of the mystery. But he planned to do it. Somehow.

The rest of the morning passed quickly with a steady succession of stomach bugs, earaches, and one sprained wrist. With each appointment, Daniel thought that Amanda was becoming more and more relaxed and sure of herself. Until the last appointment before lunch.

"Ok, who do we have here?" asked Amanda as she opened the final patient chart. "Ben Fitzgerald."

Daniel was excited to see that Ben was on the docket for the day. "I'm actually really glad you're here for this consult," he said. He stood beside Amanda and pulled the chart towards him so that they could both read it. "As you'll see from his history, Ben has really struggled with the trifecta of asthma, eczema, and food allergies. He's severely allergic to all kinds of tree nuts and milk, though his blood work has indicated that he might finally be outgrowing the milk allergy. He really should be seeing a specialist, but we don't have one in town. But with you here, maybe we can get your expert opinion."

Dimly he noticed that Amanda wasn't as excited as he was. He tried again. "Isn't this the sort of case that you said you used to see?"

"Yes, it is," she said. She stared down at the chart for a moment before she snapped it shut. "The thing is, I don't think I'm familiar enough with him to suggest the right course of treatment. You should probably handle this one."

Daniel's mouth fell open. "What?"

"I don't think I'm the right choice here. Allergies aren't like a simple ear infection, where I can prescribe an antibiotic without much prior knowledge. Allergies are very complicated and nuanced."

"I know that," Daniel said slowly. "That's why I'd like your input."

"I'm not comfortable with it. Not without more background with the patient." She spoke firmly, and

Daniel had the feeling that he wouldn't be able to change her mind. He tried to look into her eyes, to break through the wall he could feel her rebuilding, but she was clearly avoiding his gaze.

"Fine," he said after a moment. "I guess I'll see Ben."

"Great," she said briskly, handing him the chart. "I'm going to run grab some lunch. See you this afternoon."

Daniel watched in shock as she strode down the hall and out of the building, the front door swinging shut behind her with a tinkle of the bell.

What had happened to turn the competent, relatable doctor of that morning to... well, to a woman on the run? He ran over the past five minutes, trying to figure out what could have set her off, but couldn't come up with any answers.

He shook his head in confusion. Whatever else she was, Dr. Amanda Garvas was definitely a mystery.

AMANDA HID out in her hotel room over lunch. She didn't want to run the risk of running into Daniel at the diner.

She absentmindedly munched on a granola bar she'd tucked away for travelling, trying to pretend that nothing particularly important had happened that morning. Trying to block out the image of Daniel's confused face as she'd basically run away.

I'm a coward.

When her phone dinged with an email, she pulled it up eagerly. Anything was better than sitting and stewing in her own self-criticism. She'd take distraction in any form, even if it was just another request for an update from Beth.

But the email wasn't from Beth. It was from her old teacher, Dr. Kowalski.

Dear Amanda,

I was so surprised to open up my email and find the nicest note from Dr. Shane. Even better was his news that YOU were in Highland Canyon working with him! I'm delighted to hear that two of my favorite young doctors are collaborating. I know you'll learn a lot from his methods, and of course I've told him the exact same thing about you.

He mentioned you were working with the Weisman Trust now. What an exciting opportunity for you! But then, I always did know that you would go far in whatever path you chose. Whenever you have a moment, drop me a quick line and fill me in on the career path that took you there. I'm always so pleased to hear from my former students.

All the best,
Dr. K

Amanda smiled, reading the words of one of her favorite professors. Dr. Kowalski had been an unconventional figure in the Washington State medical school. She always impressed upon her students the necessity of looking at the whole person, repeatedly reminding them that patients were more than just a collection of biological systems.

Her approach tallied nicely with Amanda's religious upbringing. She knew that every patient was one of God's creatures, and having a professor with the same view kept her grounded in the middle of a competitive program.

She needed to write Dr. Kowalski back, but she shrank from having to tell her about her new career path. How could she admit to the fear she still felt? She knew her teacher would understand, but that didn't stop her from feeling ashamed.

She thought back to how she'd walked out on Daniel that morning. She knew that she owed him an explanation as well. It was a humiliating thing to do, but she knew she had to tell him the truth. It was the only way they were going to be able to work together until her work in town was done.

She sighed and stood up. If it had to be done, she might as well do it now.

DANIEL SPENT his lunch alone at his desk in the quiet office, mindlessly chewing a peanut butter and jelly sandwich while stewing over Amanda's actions that morning.

Obviously, she had some sort of hang-up about actually interacting with patients. She'd started the day as a big bundle of nerves. Her face had resembled his patients waiting to get their yearly shots – filled with dread with a dash of panic thrown in for good measure.

Still, as the day went on, he'd thought that she was starting to come around. Later in the morning, she almost seemed to be enjoying herself.

And then came Ben. Ben was a special case to Daniel. He'd taken care of the boy since he was born six years ago. He'd helped identify the food allergies that were making him sick as a baby and went on to coach his parents through the treatment of his various ailments. But Daniel was no specialist. He believed that Ben's parents, a local farming couple, should take him to someone who was better versed in the sorts of problems rooted in the immune system that Ben faced, but they hadn't yet been able to make the overnight trip.

To actually have Amanda, a specialist in just the area that Ben needed, here in the building, but unable to help, was galling. And baffling. Why wouldn't she practice the skills that she's worked so hard to learn? He'd received a glowing endorsement of Amanda from Dr. Kowalski in response to his email, so he knew she must be a good doctor. So why was she hiding out at the Weisman Trust?

Lord, he thought, *if you'd like to give me a hint, I'd appreciate it.* But nothing came to him. He'd found that more and more lately. Unanswered prayers seemed to be the norm. Possibly because he'd gotten a little slack with his own prayer life, he thought guiltily. But he pushed that train of thought aside. He was trying to figure out Amanda, not himself.

He bit into an apple, the crunch echoing in the silent room. In a few moments, the nurses would be returning from their lunch break, patients would come in for their afternoon appointments, and the noise would ratchet back up again.

And Amanda will come back, he thought. But he wasn't sure what to say to her.

He stood and started pacing around his office, wondering exactly how he should address the situation. Talk about it out the open? What if she was embarrassed? Or denied it?

Should he pretend it never happened? In the distance, he heard the tinkle of the front door. People were starting to return from lunch. He'd better figure out what he was going to say.

Back and forth. Back and forth. He felt like the tabby from the day before. Things ended well for her. Maybe he'd work this out ok, too.

As the noise from the waiting room grew, Daniel decided he couldn't wait in his office anymore. He was feeling caged. Better to wait for Amanda outside, where he could get some air.

He strode to the door and was reaching for the doorknob when suddenly it flew in toward him. He had time for one quick yelp of alarm before it slammed into his forehead and he was out cold.

When he awoke, it was with two contradictory impressions: first, a splitting headache and second, a pleasant lilac scent that he vaguely associated with Amanda. He opened his eyes and caught a glimpse of her leaning over him with a worried expression. The light seared against his eyes, though, so he had to close them again almost immediately.

"Oh, I'm so sorry," he heard Amanda say, and then the light that filtered through his eyelids went dark. Tentatively he opened his eyes again. She'd turned off the overhead fixture, leaving only his desk lamp on, and he was able to look around the room.

He was lying on the floor with his legs splayed out toward the door. He must have gone straight down when the door hit him. He groaned. Not his best moment.

"How do you feel?" Amanda asked, coming back to kneel by his side.

"Ridiculous."

The corner of Amanda's mouth went up. "I meant, physically."

"Oh. Not great."

Amanda reached out and felt his forehead, softly probing with her fingers. He relaxed against her gentle touch and closed his eyes for a moment.

"How long have I been out?"

"About ten seconds," she laughed.

"That's it? This headache is worth at least an hour unconscious."

"Yes, I think you're going to develop quite an egg on your forehead." She placed a finger just above his left eye. "Right about here."

"Ouch. Yep, that feels like the spot."

"Sorry." She pulled her phone out and turned on the flashlight. "Now look at me." He stared straight at her as she shone the light first in one eye then the other. She put the phone away, looking satisfied. "Pupils are reacting normally," she said. "How's your stomach feel? Any nausea?"

"No." He was fairly sure the butterflies he was feeling had more to do with how closely Amanda was sitting by his side than the knock on his head.

"Good." She rocked back onto her heels. "Now let's get you on your feet and make sure you don't throw up." She held out her hands and helped him to stand. He shook his head clear as Amanda continued to watch him, looking as though she were ready to grab him again if needed.

"I'm fine," he assured her.

"We'll see about that. What day is it?"

"Thursday."

"How many fingers am I holding up?"

"Four."

"Why don't you ever go eat dinner with your brother?"

"I – what?"

She laughed. "Just kidding." She crossed to the light switch. "Think you can handle it if I turn on the light?"

Daniel nodded, and squinted his eyes as light flooded the room. Slowly his eyes adjusted, and he was able to open them fully.

"Here," said Amanda, handing Daniel two pills. "Take some aspirin. You'd better get ahead of that headache that I know you have."

"Where'd you get those?"

"I'm always travel with it. Old habits, you know."

"Two aspirin," said Daniel. "Does this mean I have to call you in the morning?"

"Absolutely." She grabbed his arm and guided him to his chair. Daniel didn't feel that he needed the help, but he rather enjoyed it all the same.

"Thanks," he said.

"It's the least I could do, seeing as how I'm the one who knocked you out."

'Yeah. You sure do use some force when you open a door."

"I was in a hurry."

"Why?" Daniel asked curiously.

"Take the pills," she instructed, obviously ignoring his question, "or you'll be no good to your patients this afternoon."

He washed the medicine down with what was left of his water from lunch. "Done," he said. He blinked slowly. "So, not that I'm not glad to have your company, but why did you almost take the door off in your hurry to come in here?"

Amanda looked uncomfortable. Her green eyes looked everywhere around the room but at him. "I realized that owe you an apology. And I wanted to go ahead and get it over with."

Daniel was silent, sensing that she needed a moment to get out what she needed to say.

"This morning, with that patient –"

"Ben," he supplied.

"It's not that I didn't want to help him. It's that I just, couldn't." She swallowed visibly. "I had an unfortunate experience before I quit medicine with a case very much like his. This morning's been overwhelming, back to doing active consults and all, and then coming up on a case like Ben's." She sighed. "It was a little too real all of a sudden."

Daniel listened soberly. The kinds of feelings she was describing were familiar to anyone who'd ever practiced medicine. He didn't understand the extent of her reactions, but he could identity with the feelings behind it.

Amanda looked at him apprehensively. "In light of all that, I'd like to spend the rest of today in your office if that's ok. I need to start compiling my report for my recommendation for the Board anyway. This morning gave me a good feel for the types of cases you see, and I'd like to get it all down on paper while it's fresh in my mind."

"I thought that wasn't the plan."

"Maybe it wasn't *Beth's* plan," she said, "but since I'm the one on the ground here, I think I'm safe making the call."

You want to hide in my office, he thought. He respected the feelings she had shared, but he had his own feelings as well – primarily a strong gut reaction that hiding away wasn't the best thing for her either.

He had an idea.

"Ordinarily that would be fine," he said, "but my head really is killing me. I could really use your help this afternoon."

He could see two conflicting emotions fighting on her face. He knew she wanted to retreat to safe grant work and stay away from the patients. But he was counting on her sense of responsibility to prompt her to help him out. Not that he wanted her to feel guilty about hitting him with the door, but he was willing to take it if it got her back into visiting patients.

Amanda was opening her mouth to answer him when the phone rang suddenly. Daniel felt as if the high-pitched peal was slicing through his aching head, so he snatched it up quickly before it could ring again.

"Dr. Shane speaking."

"Hi, Daniel." Daniel recognized the voice of his sister-in-law. "What's wrong? You sound awful."

"Nothing," said Daniel, glancing at Amanda. "Just a little headache. Scratch that – a big headache. What's up?"

"Actually, I'm calling to speak to Amanda."

"Oh." Daniel was surprised. "Ok, hold on a sec." He held the phone out to Amanda who raised her eyebrows. "Sarah calling for you," he said.

Amanda took the phone. "Hi, Sarah... Really? That's so sweet of you guys... Sure, I'd love to." At that point, she turned and looked at Daniel. "I don't know about that, but I can certainly give it a try… Uh, uh… Ok, sounds good. Thanks again!"

She handed the phone back to Daniel and sat down in his spare chair.

"Well?" he asked when she didn't speak.

"Your family is so nice," she said.

"I know that. But why was she calling?"

"Sarah invited me to come to dinner tonight. Since I'm alone in town."

That sounded like Sarah, Daniel thought. She had a habit of mothering every stray in town.

"You'll enjoy that," he said. "At least if Sarah's cooking. If it's Kyle making his seven-bean chili, watch out. He's convinced it's delicious, but that stuff is deadly."

"You can help protect me. Sarah asked me to bring you."

"What?" Daniel felt put out. "Why didn't she just ask me?"

Amanda shrugged. "I don't know. But what do you say?"

"I shouldn't. I've got tons to do here. We've still got a full load of patients this afternoon, plus I haven't finished all these grant questions you gave me to do. I probably should stay here and plow through some more work."

"I'm sensing a pattern with you."

"What's that?"

"Work, work, work."

"Hey, some of that work was assigned by you."

"I know. But as your doctor –"

"My doctor?"

"Yes, your doctor who is keeping an eye on your for signs of concussion, I think it would be best if you took tonight off from work and came with me."

Daniel sighed. "What if it's Kyle's chili?"

Amanda cracked a smile. "Then we'll eat light and go out afterwards for ice cream and Tums."

Daniel considered. "Maybe I can propose a deal. I'll go with you tonight if you go on my rounds with me this afternoon."

"Oh, I don't know about that, Daniel."

Daniel smiling, liking the sound of her using his name. "As my doctor, I thought it was your duty to stay with me and make sure I'm not concussed."

Amanda crossed her arms.

"So you're playing that card, hmm?"

"Only if you are."

Amanda looked at him with one eyebrow raised for a moment. Finally, she threw her hands up in the air. "Fine. You win."

He grinned. "Then I guess it's a date."

CHAPTER 5

Daniel locked his office that evening in a cheerful mood, unaccountably excited for what was, after all, just an ordinary dinner at his brother's house.

The rest of the afternoon had gone fairly well. True to her word, Amanda went with him to see all his patients. Assuming she didn't chicken out again, Daniel was perfectly willing to let Amanda see some patients on her own on Monday. Whether or not Amanda was ready for that, he didn't yet know. After they'd ushered out the last patient of the day, she'd gone back to her hotel to get ready for dinner. Daniel wasn't sure what she needed to do, but he was happy to close up the office himself, promising to pick her up in one hour so that she didn't have to find the way on the dark Montana roads.

He still had a slight headache, but the aspirin had helped. Well, either that, or the memory of Amanda's cool fingers on his head. He couldn't be sure, but it certainly felt like she'd shown more than the ordinary concern a doctor would show for her patient.

So, yes, on the whole he was looking forward to tonight. That feeling was only heightened when he first saw Amanda. She must have been waiting for him in the hotel lobby, because she stepped out onto the sidewalk right as he arrived.

Daniel blinked.

She'd changed clothes. Gone was the professional attire of the day, and in its place was a simple white sundress with a dark purple cardigan. Her dark hair was down and loose, unlike her usual businesslike bun. He had the craziest urge to reach out and touch it.

"Wow," he said before thinking. "You look beautiful."

She looked surprised but pleased. "Thanks."

He swallowed. It was going to be difficult tonight to remember his resolution to focus on work. In his mind, he still knew that he had to prioritize the new clinic above all else. Ethan needed it. But his heart was starting to wonder, would it be possible to have the clinic and something more?

She was looking at him with a questioning expression, and he realized he had frozen.

"Sorry," he said. "Ready to go?"

"Hold on." She came right up to him so quickly that Daniel had no time to wonder what she was doing. She reached her hand up and stroked his forehead. He held perfectly still, overcome by surprise and another feeling he was harder pressed to name.

She frowned. "You're swelling more now. Did you remember to ice it?"

Right. He's almost forgotten about his accident earlier in the day. "Not exactly. I got distracted with some patient files."

She sighed and shook her head. "You need to take care of yourself."

He smiled. "Why, when I've got you?" He noticed the softening of her eyes and inwardly exulted. "Come on," he said. "We'd better get going. My truck's right over here." He guided her back across the street to his practice's parking lot, just barely managing to keep himself from placing his hand on her back to lead her. He kept glancing at her, almost unable to believe that he'd be spending the evening with someone like her.

He opened the cab door for her, and she smiled her thanks. On the way back around to his door, he took a few deep breaths to steady himself.

He'd been kidding when he'd called this a date earlier in the day. But now he wasn't so sure.

THE RIDE over was quiet, though Amanda wasn't quite sure why. Daniel seemed oddly tongue-tied compared with his usual relaxed manner. She was content though to look out the window at the gorgeous scenery in the fading light of the day. It really was a change from her home of Seattle, but she loved the wide-open grasslands and hills in the distance. She found herself wondering if she could ever live in a place like this.

She stopped herself short. Now what had put that thought into her head? She glanced sideways at Daniel. It was a good thing she had that work rule to guide her. No dating grantees. Not that she wanted to anyways, she told herself. What would happen to her career at the Trust out here in the wilds of the west?

"Here we are," Daniel announced after fifteen minutes. They'd pulled up in front of a cute little bungalow with white lace curtains at all the windows. He turned off the car and turned to face Amanda. "Are you ready for chaos?"

"Bring it on," said Amanda, climbing out of the cab.

And it was chaotic at first. Daniel let themselves into the house with a knock to announce their presence, but no one would have heard it anyways. The small house was bursting with noise. To the right, Amanda could see into the kitchen through a cutout in the wall where Sarah was dressed in a striped apron, her long blond hair pulled back into a messy ponytail. She was fiddling with oven knobs, but she waved a spoon in greeting as soon as she noticed them. "Sorry it's so loud," she shouted. "We're getting close to bedtime."

Straight ahead was the source of all the racket. Kyle was in the couple's living room trying to soothe two crying babies at once, both of whom definitely wanted attention.

"Not to worry. Reinforcements have arrived," Daniel shouted over the din. He grabbed Amanda's hand and led her farther into the house towards Kyle.

"Praise the Lord," said Kyle when he saw them.

Daniel scooped up Ethan and turned and deposited him straight into Amanda's arms. She received him with surprise, but was willing. Ethan stopped crying almost immediately, seemingly glad to be with someone who would give him her full attention.

"Hey, buddy," she murmured, gently bouncing him up and down in her arms.

Meanwhile, Daniel picked up Robert and playfully turned him upside down above his head so that they were eye to eye. When Robert found himself within inches of his uncle's face, he stopped crying as well.

The sudden silence was almost as alarming as the noise had been moments earlier.

Kyle gave an enormous sigh of relief. "Am I glad you two are here."

Daniel placed Robert up high on his head, where the baby perched like a mini-Superman, his uncle stabilizing his little body with one hand on each side. Daniel looked from right to left while the baby giggled. "Was someone yelling in here? I thought I heard something." He flipped Robert down into his arms. "Oh, hey! Was it you?"

Amanda watched him, her health melting. He really was so good with these boys. When Daniel caught her eye a moment later, she feared that some of her thoughts might have been showing in her face. His eyes suddenly grew more intense on hers, and it was as if they were the only two people in the room.

Kyle cleared his throat and broke the spell.

Amanda felt her face burning. "Excuse me," she said. "I think Ethan and I will see what's going on in the kitchen."

She retreated down the hall toward the kitchen as quickly as she could without jostling Robert.

Sarah was bustling around the kitchen.

"Hi, Amanda," she smiled. "I'm so glad you could come to dinner tonight."

"Me, too. Thank you for inviting me." Amanda looked around the room. There was a pot of what looked like potato soup simmering on the stove and some lettuce leaves drying on the counter. "Can I do anything to help?" she asked.

Sarah pushed a strand of blond hair out of her eyes. "Trust me, you are helping. Keeping the babies happy is the biggest challenge while making dinner."

That was an area where Amanda was more than happy to help. Ethan nestled comfortably into her arms, laying his head on her shoulder.

Sarah smiled and stopped her work briefly to rub the baby's back. "My tired boy. I think he likes you."

"The feeling's mutual," Amanda said, nuzzling her cheek against the top of Ethan's head. Before she'd left medicine, she'd worked with some individuals with Down syndrome, and she'd always felt that they were some of her sweetest patients. This was her first experience with a baby with the syndrome, however, and she found that combo between the characteristic sweetness and general baby cuteness was a powerful combination. No wonder Daniel felt such a pull to protect this little guy.

Amanda swayed gently back and forth with Ethan while Sarah went back to tossing the salad. She could barely hear Kyle and Daniel's voices drifting in from the kitchen, with an occasional squeal contributed by Robert. Amanda smiled, imagining that Daniel was probably flipping him upside down again.

"Do you like tomatoes?" Sarah asked, pausing with her salad tongs in midair.

"Love them," said Amanda.

"Then I'll add some to the salad. We had a really nice harvest from our garden this year. Daniel couldn't get enough of them. It was one of the few things that would convince him to stop working for a little bit and come eat with us."

"He works long hours, doesn't he?"

Sarah rolled her eyes. "Long doesn't cover it. He used to be better at balancing work and fun, but the last couple of years, he's pushed himself harder and harder." She glanced up at Amanda briefly. "Though he hasn't come out and said it, I think he feels like he's got to put his whole life on hold until the new clinic is up and running. We were getting worried about him, but he doesn't listen to us."

"Is that why you made me ask him to come tonight?" asked Amanda.

Sarah looked slightly guilty. "Let's just say that we thought he might find it harder to say no to you than to us. I hope you don't mind."

Amanda laughed quietly. "No, I don't mind. That's actually something I encounter in work a lot. Since I'm a representative of the Trust, potential grantees feel like they have to say yes to every idea I have. It can be tough to get an honest opinion." She felt the baby on her shoulder relaxing more and more, so she kept her voice low. "But not Daniel. He drove a hard bargain to come tonight."

"Maybe he did," said Sarah, "but that was probably for show." She glanced at Amanda slyly as she pulled water glasses from a cabinet. "I'm sure you've picked up on this, but I think Daniel is interested in you."

"What?" said Amanda so forcefully that Ethan stirred against her. She instantly started soothing him but her mind was elsewhere. This was a challenge she hadn't expected. Was Sarah right? She thought back quickly over their recent interactions. He'd been friendly, even very friendly, but that was it. And, ok, this evening she was pretty sure that Daniel had appreciated her appearance when he picked her up, and, yes, they did just have some sort of moment in the living room. But he had also been almost completely silent on the ride over, and that hardly seemed like the action of a man who was falling for her.

"I'm sorry," said Sarah with a concerned expression. "I didn't mean to startle you. And I might be wrong anyway." She began to fill the glasses with water. "It's just been a while since Daniel's pulled his head out of his practice and looked at the people around him. He hasn't had time for fun. Or himself. Or even for God. But he's seemed different the last couple of days. I feel like it started when you came to town."

Amanda cleared her throat. "I doubt it has anything to do with me. I haven't... I mean, he hasn't..."

Sarah came over and laid a hand on her arm. "Don't worry about it. I shouldn't have said anything. I never meant to make you feel uncomfortable."

"No, it's fine," said Amanda. "It's just that," she cleared her throat, "we're not really allowed to date grantees."

Sarah's eyebrows went up. "Oh," she said in surprise.

"It's a question of credibility," Amanda went on. "The Board has to trust our recommendations, and if personal feelings become involved..." She trailed off.

Sarah nodded. "I hadn't thought about it, but I suppose that does make a lot of sense."

"Sarah," Amanda heard a deep voice. She turned in surprise. Daniel stood in the doorway of the kitchen, a funny expression on his face.

Oh, Lord, did he hear what we were talking about?

Judging by the way Daniel avoided her eyes, she guessed that the answer was yes. She cringed inwardly. She must have sounded so arrogant, as if she were convinced that he had feelings for her!

"Kyle wanted to know if he should go ahead and throw the boys in the bath."

Sarah checked the time. "That's a good idea." She looked at Amanda and Ethan. "On second thought, why don't you tell him just to bathe Robert? It looks like Ethan's already passed out for the night."

Amanda's eyes widened as she heard the tiniest of snore. "He fell asleep on me?" Amanda asked, twisting her body so that Sarah could see Ethan's face.

"He sure did," said Sarah. "You're a baby whisperer." She smiled at her snoozing boy. "Want me to take him to his crib?"

Amanda shook her head, loving the feel of the snuggly infant. "Finish up what you're doing. I don't mind holding him."

"In that case, I'm going to help with Robert. Kyle has a tendency to let bath time go on for an hour, and we'll never get to sit down for dinner." She pulled off her apron and threw it on the counter. "Be right back."

Amanda slowly rubbed circles on the little boy's back and tried to look as if she were unaffected by Daniel's serious gaze. He leaned against the doorjamb, watching her with a look in his brown eyes that she couldn't quite place.

"I've never held a baby like this before," Amanda said quietly. The experience was so soothing, and, yet, it also made her yearn for something, for a different kind of life than she currently had. Snuggling Ethan, she marveled anew that her own Lord had come into the world as a baby. This moment in the quiet kitchen drove home how vulnerable people really were. And how much they needed care and attention. Care and attention that she used to be able to give.

"You look right at home," said Daniel. "Happy."

"I am happy. Who wouldn't be with this guy for company?"

Daniel held her gaze for a moment, and something unspoken hung on the air between them. She waited in fear for him to mention her conversation with Sarah

Finally, he said, "If you're good in here, I'm going to step outside real quick. I noticed a couple of wasps nests on the way in that I can get rid of for them. They're so busy with the kids that they miss stuff like that."

"Daniel Shane, always working," Amanda murmured, but she smiled.

He gave a sort of grimace in return before he left the room.

Amanda looked after him in confusion.

Now what had that been about?

WALKING OUT the front door, Daniel cursed himself for his stupidity. He hadn't meant to walk in on Sarah and Amanda having what was obviously a private conversation, but once he had, it wasn't like he could unhear it.

So, Amanda wasn't allowed to date grantees?

He guessed that put him out of the running completely.

What was he talking about? he asked himself. It wasn't like he was going to ask her out or anything. Sure, she looked beautiful tonight, but that was no reason to throw away all his plans. He had a new clinic to open. It was going to take all his time and effort, just like it had for the past two years.

As Daniel took care of the wasps nests, he wondered grumpily if there had been other grantees whom Amanda had wanted to date. Why did they have the rule if nothing had happened in the past?

He walked to the backyard to check for any more stray nests. On the way, he shook his head at himself. Honestly, he was jealous of some *hypothetical* grantee who Amanda *might* have possibly liked. None of it was even real! He had to get a hold of himself.

Kyle and Sarah had a quaint gazebo in their backyard that Kyle had built by hand shortly after their marriage. Daniel had always liked the spot, and he knew that Kyle and Sarah loved to eat out in it during the summertime. They called it their quiet oasis in the midst of the sheer pandemonium of raising twins.

But the lovely spot did nothing tonight to calm his spirit, as he ruthlessly cleared another wasp nest that he discovered in the rafters. He had no idea why he was so on edge.

"Daniel!" he heard Kyle call from the house. "Stop working and get in here to eat."

"Coming," he yelled back. He took a quick look at his handiwork. If he hadn't been able to clear Amanda from his thoughts, at least he'd managed to get something done.

He glanced back at the house, lit up in the darkness. He could see the others through the light curtains, talking and laughing.

Time to come out of the dark and put a smile on. He could do it.

One hour later, Daniel pushed himself back from the table with a groan. "Sarah, as usual, that was awesome. And I'm stuffed." He'd always enjoyed Sarah's potato soup and homemade rolls, and tonight the company had made the meal even more pleasant than usual.

"Delicious meal, honey," echoed Kyle.

"I couldn't agree more," said Amanda. "Honestly, you guys eat like kings in this town. Between this and the diner, I can't believe my good luck." She dabbed the corner of her mouth with a napkin. "I'm not going to be able to fit into my clothes by the end of my visit."

"It was nothing," said Sarah. "But I'm glad you enjoyed it."

"I wanted to cook dinner," Kyle announced from the head of the table. "I was going to make chili. But for some reason Sarah wouldn't let me."

Daniel spoke. "You wanted to feed us, right? Not send us back to the doctor's office."

Kyle swatted at Daniel's head, and Amanda laughed.

"Hey, don't take his side," Daniel said threateningly to Amanda. "He's already got a whole house of people on Team-Kyle."

"Sorry," said Amanda with a twinkle in her eye. "Kyle, don't pick on your brother."

"You know he's the older one, right?" Kyle teased.

Daniel reached out to cuff Kyle's head this time and was rewarded by another musical laugh from Amanda.

Sarah stood to start gathering plates from the table, and Kyle immediately jumped up to help her. He slid his arm around his wife's shoulder and planted a loud kiss on her cheek. Sarah rolled her eyes, but laughed.

"Get to work," she said, stacking plates.

"Let us help," said Amanda, standing up.

"No, we've got it, I promise," said Kyle. In a pretend whisper he added, "Sarah will kill me if I let you help. She says guests should get to rest, not do our dishes."

"I heard that," said Sarah. She turned to Amanda. "But it is true. You guys did enough with the babies."

Daniel leaned back, happy to take his sister-in-law's order as she and her husband left the room. Amanda was seated across from his at the table, all the better for him to talk and laugh with her throughout the meal. Now, alone with her, he studied her face. He'd spent the last three days in Amanda's company, yet he felt as though he was seeing her with fresh eyes tonight. She looked younger and more vulnerable now that she wasn't on duty. Seeing her with Ethan, too, had opened up a whole new way of viewing her. When she was cuddling the baby, Daniel got a glimpse of what she would be like as a mother. And it was a very pleasant image.

Of course, now that he knew her stance on dating grantees, it was a pleasant image that he needed to stamp out. However much Daniel's feelings had been growing, there was no future for them. He couldn't risk the grant.

She met his eyes and smiled at him, but didn't speak. Daniel saw that her hand was resting on the table by her glass, and, once he noticed that hand, he suddenly couldn't think of anything else. He had an overwhelming urge to reach out and hold it. Would she let him? Even better, did she want him to? Daniel felt as if his whole world were tied up in this one question, this one chance to reach out right now and touch her.

Stop it! he told himself. *She is not available. Not to you anyway.*

Kyle and Sarah chose that exact moment to walk in bearing dessert, and Daniel breathed a sigh of relief. Peeking at Amanda's face, he had no way of knowing if she'd suspected what was in his mind. He hoped that she hadn't, since it was breaking his resolution of, what, only an hour ago?

He groaned quietly. It was going to be tougher to keep everything professional than he thought.

WHEN AMANDA climbed back into the truck for the ride home, she couldn't help but shiver in the dropped temperature. The Montana summer had a definite chilly side, much more so than the weather she'd be experiencing in Seattle right now.

Daniel immediately turned up the heat, and Amanda smiled at his thoughtfulness. Of course he noticed that she was cold. And how like him to fix the problem without making a big deal out of it.

"Did you have a good time?" he asked her as he pulled down the road.

"Wonderful," she assured him. "Your family is great."

"They're not so bad."

"You can tell they like to serve others. They're like you in that way."

Daniel glanced at her. "What do you mean?" he asked, sounding genuinely curious.

"Well, you've got your brother and his wife, basically inviting a total stranger into their home because she didn't have anywhere else to go. And you serve people all day long every day."

Daniel laughed. "Don't make me out to be some sort of hero."

"I'm not making you out to be anything. I'm only describing you the way you are." She shrugged. "I can hardly go anywhere in this town without people telling me how great you are."

"I seriously doubt that."

"Oh yeah?" Amanda liked a challenge. She ticked off on her fingers as she talked. "Millie positively gushed about how you've helped Rita with her speech problems."

"Any doctor would do the same."

"On my way out of the hotel this morning, an older woman stopped to tell me how you treated her grandson for free."

"That must have been Christine Walters. She's a sweetheart."

"And the waitress who took my card this morning insisted that you were the only doctor her child would see without throwing a fit."

"Is this stuff relevant to your report?"

"Everything's relevant," Amanda said shortly, rather enjoying putting him on the spot. "I'm just saying, it seems like you do a lot of good for your patients. And that's not even counting all the work you've put in the new clinic, on top of your current practice. It's a lot."

Daniel shrugged. "It's got to be done. You know as well as I do the kind of medical interventions that Ethan is likely to need as he gets older. I have the ability to help with that. I've got to do it."

Amanda hesitated, wondering if she should bring up a topic that had been on her mind that evening. She took a deep breath and decided to go for it. "But do you have to do it alone?"

Daniel looked at her questioningly. "I'm not sure what you're getting at."

Amanda bit her lip. "Sarah mentioned earlier that you've been working so hard that you haven't had time for yourself or for, well, for God. I just think it would help you to remember that you are not alone."

"Is God going to open the clinic for me?"

Amanda gave him an exasperated look. "Not exactly. But you don't have to do this all on your own strength alone. You know that right?"

Daniel was quiet for a moment. "Kyle's my little brother, Amanda. And although I know we're grown up now, and he's his own man, I still feel like it's my job to protect him. That's what big brothers do."

Amanda sat quietly, listening, and he went on.

"When Kyle and Sarah found out that Ethan had Down syndrome, I heard that as my call from God to help them. I knew what kind of medical clinic we needed to build, and so I had to do it. *I* had to do it." He looked at her briefly before turning back to the road. "I'm not sure how to put it into words." He ran his hands through his hair again in that gesture that Amanda loved.

"Don't you trust God to help you?" Amanda asked quietly.

"Maybe. I don't know. I'd rather trust myself."

Amanda looked out the window as the road rumbled under their feet. She thought about how Daniel had reached out to the Weisman Trust for the financial help to build the clinic. He'd recognized that he couldn't do that part of it alone. Maybe he wasn't quite as stubbornly self-sufficient as he thought he was. He only needed a little time to see it.

They'd reached the hotel. Daniel parked the car in front, but Amanda didn't move to get out. She felt drawn to stay there with him if only for a few more minutes.

"I had a lovely time," she said. "I'm glad you took the night off to come with me. And I know Kyle and Sarah were, too."

He laughed. "Yeah, they're always after me to take some time off. Find a nice girl, settle down, and come to weekly dinners."

Amanda chose her words carefully. "And that doesn't sound good to you?"

"Maybe," said Daniel, not meeting her eyes. "With the right woman. But not right now. There's too much to do."

"I see," said Amanda. Her conversation with Sarah felt doubly embarrassing now. He clearly wasn't interested in her at all. She pushed open the door. "Thanks for the ride."

"Anytime. Have a good night."

Amanda stood back under the awning of the inn, as Daniel backed out and drove down the street. She closed her eyes. For a night that had started so nicely, why did it feel like everything had ended wrong?

CHAPTER 6

Daniel couldn't help but feel awkward the next morning. His conversation with Amanda on the way home had touched on some truths he did his best not to think about. How funny that she could see straight to the heart of his struggles, his challenges to trust in God for what he needed.

And then there was the end of the conversation. Daniel passed his hand over his eyes. In his worry to convince Amanda that he wasn't going to violate her no-dating rule, he was afraid he'd overdone it. He'd sounded downright cold, and his words had replayed in his head on repeat while he was trying to fall asleep.

Well, however Amanda did or did not feel about him, she obviously wasn't going to let it interfere with work. And neither would he. Not now that he knew it could jeopardize the grant for the new clinic. He thought of Kyle and Sarah and how they were depending on him. This grant was just too important. Ethan was too important.

So, when Amanda came in for the day, looking self-conscious and embarrassed herself, he did his best to put on a normal face.

They spent the morning together again. Daniel asked her if she'd like to see patients without him, but she said no so emphatically that he didn't press her. So they were in and out of patient rooms all morning, consulting with each other between visits. The arrangement actually worked out pretty well for them. It was hard to stay awkward with each other while they were focused on meeting the needs of his patients.

By lunchtime, Daniel was feeling almost normal again, and, by her more relaxed demeanor, he guessed that she was, too. He was relieved to know that he hadn't seriously damaged their working relationship the night before.

At his invitation, she'd set up in his office over lunch. She'd brought in her laptop, saying that she wanted to get started on her report to the Trust. He had a sneaking suspicion that she actually had planned for a way to fill her time, in case things were weird between them. If that was her original motivation though, it looked to have disappeared after their morning together. She welcomed his presence with a smile.

For his part, he sat down to preview patient files for that afternoon's cases. Propping his feet up on the front side of his desk, he was surprised to feel how relaxed they were after the events of the night before. They worked in a comfortable silence, occasionally breaking it to throw out a thought or comment to the other.

"You have a fairly high percentage of patients without health insurance," she remarked at one point.

Daniel looked up from the chart of an infant he'd be examining later that day and thought about her question. "That's fairly common around here. People are much more likely to self-insure rather than rely on employment-based insurance. Plus there are lots of family farms in the area and even more ranchers. Those aren't occupations that typically come with benefits."

"I suppose not." Amanda typed for a moment. "And how do you expect that to affect the new medical center's budget? Expenses will be higher at the clinic than they are now."

Daniel laughed. "Just because patient self-insure doesn't mean they don't pay their bills. We're a self-reliant people out here. We don't run away from our debts."

Amanda lifted on corner of her mouth. "I think you know I wasn't suggesting that."

"I know," said Daniel. "And you're right, there are a few patients who are unable to pay. But, as you'll remember from the budget, part of the grant will go towards a patient fund, to enable us to provide some free or low-cost healthcare to people on a sliding scale."

Amanda nodded and resumed typing her notes, and Daniel went back to his charts. Flipping to the next one, he noticed an upcoming patient that might be an issue for Amanda.

He cleared his throat. "Just a heads-up, we've got another allergy case coming in this afternoon. It's fairly straightforward. He's only in maintenance mode, but I, uh, thought you might want to know."

Amanda didn't lift her eyes from her computer screen, but he heard her stop typing. "And why would you think I'd want to know that ahead of time?" she asked.

Daniel hesitated on how to answer, but, in the end, decided to go with a direct answer. "Because when I asked for your expertise on Ben Fitzgerald's case, you… well, you freaked out."

Amanda did look up at that. "I did not freak out."

Daniel cocked his head. "Yeah. You did."

"I declined to do the consult."

"You abruptly left once you heard the details of his case."

Amanda sat in silence, and Daniel assumed the subject was closed. He resumed examining his patient files, but looked up in surprise a moment later when Amanda began speaking.

"It's possible that allergy patients might be a sort of... trigger for me," she said.

"Yeah, I picked up on that," he said slowly. He raised his eyebrows. "Care to share why?"

Amanda fidgeted under his gaze and began twirling a strand of shiny, smooth hair around her index finger.

She really is nervous, he thought. *What happened to make her feel this way?*

She abruptly stopped spinning her finger and instead folded her hands together, clenched tightly in her lap.

"I spent five years working with patients with food allergies, and I really loved my work," she began. She looked up at the ceiling and almost sounded as if she were reciting from memory. He wondered how many times she'd gone over this in her own brain.

"It was so rewarding," she was saying, "helping people manage what can be a very difficult condition. I had this one patient named Steve. Steve was seven years old." She smiled to herself. "He was such a sweetheart. He used to bring his matchbox cars from home and go around leaving them in all the patient rooms. He said he wanted the kids to have toys to play with." She smiled. "It would drive the nurses crazy, finding those little cars all over the place when we were trying to close up."

Daniel laughed.

"But he was one of my favorite patients. I guess you're not supposed to have favorites, but I did. He was an awesome kid. Anyways, he had tons of allergies. I mean, tons. The poor guy – I think he survived on chicken and straight veggies for his entire childhood. I'd been treating him for years, and, over time, his bloodwork was definitely improving. It looked like he was finally going to be able to try wheat, so I scheduled him for a food challenge."

She looked at Daniel. "It was a run-of-the-mill challenge. We gave him progressively more bread over the course of two hours and monitored his reaction. Something I've done with at least 100 other patients over the years." She sighed. "He was doing so well. Laughing and cutting up right until the end, when he suddenly went into anaphylactic shock."

Daniel listened soberly, knowing how serious anaphylaxis could be.

"We did absolutely everything we could at the clinic. Pumped him full of epi-pens and antihistamines and steroids. But we couldn't get it under control."

"Did he…" Daniel had trouble getting the question out, but Amanda seemed to understand.

"He made it," she said quietly, "praise God, but not without a lengthy stay in the ICU." She rubbed her hand on the back of her neck. "But it really shook me. No, more than that. It shook my whole foundation."

Daniel frowned. "You know you didn't do anything wrong, right? The food challenge was a reasonable thing to do in that situation."

"I know I didn't." She leaned forward. "But that's the thing. It was almost a terrible outcome – Steven almost died – and I hadn't even made a mistake! How much borrowed time was I on before I did make a mistake, and one of my patients paid the price for it? How long until I missed a serious symptom or accidentally prescribed the wrong dose of medicine or pushed ahead on a food challenge before my patient was ready?"

Daniel was silent. She had a point. It was a fear that he'd found all doctors had to live with.

"After Steven's incident, I just didn't have it in me anymore. I started looking for a way to leave active medicine. I had a connection at the Weisman Trust through a colleague, and it seemed like the natural next step." She held up her hands in a shrug. "And the rest, as they say, is history."

"Don't you miss it?" asked Daniel.

"Sometimes. But it's not worth the uncertainty. It's not worth getting attached to patients, only to run the risk of hurting them somehow." She tapped her computer and gave a wry smile. "Grant work is safer."

Daniel watched her thoughtfully as Amanda went back to typing. This definitely gave some insight into her behavior the past few days – her unwillingness to engage with patients in the beginning, and, more recently, her desire to have him accompany her on all the consults.

She no longer trusted her own skills, Daniel realized. Or her own heart.

AMANDA SPENT the weekend holed up in her hotel room, crafting her report that she would use to convince the Trust to approve Daniel's grant. She ventured out only for take-out meals from the diner and church on Sunday morning. By asking at the front desk of the Inn, she found a church within easy walking distance. Sliding into a smooth wooden pew in the back, she spotted Daniel sitting with his brother and family near a side door. She almost tried to catch him after the service to say hello, but, after a moment's reflection, she opted to give him his space. She felt a little self-conscious after talking to Daniel about his relationship with God the other night. After the fact, she realized with embarrassment that she probably had sounded like a self-righteous know-it-all. The last thing she wanted was for Daniel to think she was keeping tabs on him at church.

After her quiet weekend, Amanda felt mentally prepared to try and tackle another week with patients. And although she still felt the old fear rising up now and again, on the whole she started to feel like she was hitting her stride. She was becoming more comfortable in the pediatrician's office and was seeing some patients on her own now. Whenever she came up against a tricky case, however, she was glad to let Daniel handle it. He always did so without a word of criticism, something that Amanda appreciated. She was glad she'd finally shared the story about Steven. Sure, maybe it didn't show her in the best light as a doctor, but at least now she didn't have to keep hiding why she didn't want to see too many patients.

Amanda was very pleased with how the report was coming along. She'd always had a good memory, something that came in very handy during medical school. Now she used it to gather details about Daniel's practice throughout the day and add them to her report by night. She herself was convinced that the Trust should award the grant and she was doing her best to convey that through the report. You never knew what detail was going to strike a chord with the Trust Board members, so she wanted to be thorough.

The following weekend rolled around, and a bright Saturday morning found Amanda making the short walk over to Daniel's office. She'd originally planned on spending this weekend much like the last – only her, her computer, some tasty take-out, and her pink pajamas. But on Friday, Daniel had mentioned that she should come by the office the next morning.

"Why?" she asked.

Daniel smiled mysteriously. "Just check it out. 9:00." He held up one hand like he was swearing. "I promise it's work-related. And it'll be fun."

So here she was, along with, she saw, several other people. There were ten or so cars in the parking spaces in front of the doctor's office, and she could see a crowd of people through the front windows of the building.

Intrigued, Amanda hurried ahead.

When she opened the front door, she was greeted by a wave of excited chatter from a group of kids and their parents inside.

The waiting room had been rearranged since the previous evening. All the chairs were lined up along the walls, with a large area cleared in the middle. There were two folding tables set up at low heights for children. One was covered with smocks, paint sets, brushes, and canvases, while the other held brightly colored clay in various colors and even two small potter's wheels.

She spotted Daniel across the room, talking to Millie. Rita was running around the room with some friends, but she stopped when she came across Amanda.

"Hi," she said with a smile. "I remember you. You helped Dr. Shane save my kittens."

Amanda squatted down to be on the same level. She was both pleased that Rita had remembered her and amazed at how outgoing Rita seemed this morning. She'd been so quiet and shy when she'd brought in her cat. "That's me. Although Dr. Shane did most of the work. How are your kittens?"

"They're all growing," said Rita, stumbling slightly over her words. "Except Bella. She's the mommy cat. But mom says they are all doing good. I get to keep them." She held up her fingers. "I have five cats now."

"That's a pretty big jump from zero," said Amanda. "You've got a nice mommy."

"I know."

"Rita!" called a little boy from across the room. "Come play!"

"Ok!" yelled Rita. She waved back at Amanda as she darted to the other kids.

Amanda stood up and caught Daniel's eye. He motioned for her to come over and join him and Millie.

"You came!" said Daniel when she reached them, the warmth of his expression making clear just how welcome she was.

"Of course, I did," said Amanda, flushing under his gaze. "But I've got to ask, what is going on?"

Millie laughed. "This is the secret of Dr. Shane's success. You'd think it was his excellent patient care, but really, it's that he provides a way to keep the kids busy and happy on a Saturday morning." She sighed. "I've tried to convince him to do it more than once a month."

"So this is a regular thing?"

Daniel nodded. "Sure is. We switch in and out with different art teachers who volunteer their time to work with the kids."

"It's been great for Rita," said Millie, watching her daughter across the room. "It's really helped her to have a low-stress environment to interact with other kids. She's with a babysitter during the week, but this is pure playtime for her. It's helped her force herself to speak more which has improved her speech impediments. She gets so excited for it."

"Yes," said Amanda, "I noticed how bubbly she was this morning."

"She loves it." Millie made a face, watching Rita play tag across the waiting room. "But now she's maybe a little too exuberant. I'd better go talk to her before she knocks over some paint."

She hurried off, and Amanda shifted so that she could speak to Daniel and watch the room.

"So, what inspired you to do this?" she asked, watching the kids milling about.

"It was a technique that I learned from Dr. Kowalski last year. We tried it out last fall, and it worked so well we kept right on doing it every four weeks." He leaned back against the wall, watching the children. "Kids are able to relax when they're being artistic, and the morning serves all sorts of medical goals." He started keeping track on his fingers. "One, it allows kids to be creative and express their feelings, something that's been invaluable for my patients who are doing through some sort of emotional upheaval, be it a move, divorce, grief, what-have-you. As I'm sure you guessed, we only have a couple mental health specialists in town, and none that focus on adolescents, so this is my way to help fill that gap.

"Second, I've got some patients who really need to see an occupational therapist – not that we have any in town, once again – and the art projects give a good way to work on their fine motor skills. While the kids are creating their masterpieces, I usually talk with those parents one-on-one to give them exercises that they can do at home."

"And third is perhaps the most important reason at all."

Amanda looked at him curiously. "What's that?"

He grinned. "It's really fun."

Right then a woman in blue overalls clapped her hands for everyone's attention.

"It's starting," said Daniel. "Sit back and enjoy."

As the lady corralled the kids and got them started working on various projects, Amanda slowly prowled around the room to observe. She saw children working intently on various projects. One boy unconsciously stuck his tongue out as he molded a lump of blue clay into a horse, and an older girl was allowed to try out the potter's wheel. When what was starting to look like a bowl suddenly went flying off the wheel, they all broke out into immediate laughter. Amanda joined in with a few other parents to gather up the pieces of clay for her to start again.

"Happens every time," whispered Millie to her.

The budding artist grinned and started back to work.

Amanda loved the energy in the room. All the children seemed to be having fun, and she enjoyed watching them work.

Mostly, though, her eyes followed Daniel. She watched as he knelt next to a small girl who was painting. He said something to her that made her giggle. Then he moved on to a boy who looked to be in kindergarten. Daniel reached out and unobtrusively corrected the boy's grip on his paintbrush. He clapped the boy on the back gently and moved on as the child wrinkled his forehead in concentration.

Amanda noticed that Daniel also used the time to speak with all of the parents. Some he simply exchanged friendly greetings with. With others, he had longer conversations, his expression earnest as he discussed some observation or treatment plan with them.

She found herself wondering, where did this man come from? He was so kind and cared so much. She'd never met anyone like him before.

And she was torn. She knew she wanted her career at the Trust. Professionally, it was the only path left open to her. She couldn't leave it.

But on the other hand, she felt so drawn to Daniel, a pull that was only becoming stronger with every day she spent with him. The more she knew him, the more she was starting to feel for him. She could almost see her carefully built defenses falling into pieces around her.

God, she silently prayed, *guide me. Please, guide me.*

TWO HOURS later, Daniel lifted two chairs back into position in the waiting room.

"Thanks for staying to help clean up," he said to Amanda. They were the only two left after the crazy morning.

"My pleasure," she said. She was kneeling on the floor, picking up stray dots of clay and mashing them into one big ball.

Over the past week, he'd felt that they had moved past his moment of weakness when he'd asked her out. They had a good working relationship going now, and every day the grant was looking to be more and more a certainty. By this time next year, there was every reason to believe that the new clinic would be finished and operational. It was just what he wanted.

And yet, for some reason, he had to remind himself of that all the time. In his head, he knew he wanted the clinic above all else, and that nothing should distract from that.

But his heart… well, his heart was telling him a different story.

He paused in his tidying to watch Amanda. She had a serious expression on her face as she worked, as though there was no way she was going to let a stray bit of clay escape her. He couldn't help but laugh as she snaked her upper body underneath a chair to fish out a glob of red.

"Don't get stuck under there," he said.

She pulled herself out and smiled at him, the red clay added to her growing ball of castaways. "The day I get stuck under a chair is the day I go on a diet."

"If you dieted there'd be nothing left," he said without thinking. "You're already perfect."

She blushed, and he turned away quickly. When would he learn to put a filter on himself?

Daniel surveyed the room. "That was the fastest clean-up after one of those things I've ever had. The second pair of hands makes a big difference."

"Glad I could help," said Amanda.

"I've only got to move the last folding table to the back storage closet, and I think we'll be in good shape."

"Let me help," she said.

"No, I've got it. It's not too heavy. I already moved one."

She walked over to the table and took one edge. "You just said two pairs of hands makes a difference. So let my hands help."

Daniel didn't have a good answer for that, so he took the other end. Together they lifted it and walked it back down the hall to where the walk-in supply closet stood open.

"To your left there," Daniel directed. "Right up against the wall."

Carefully, they leaned the table back into position along the back wall.

"Thanks," said Daniel. "Now we're all ready for next month."

Amanda was surveying the small space. "You've almost got more art supplies in here than medical supplies."

Daniel laughed. "This is only my backup storage space. As much as I like art day, I do actually keep medical equipment in the office as well." He watched Amanda run her finger along a shelf full of wooden dowels and glitter. He shifted, suddenly aware of how close they were standing to each other.

Amanda turned to him. "I heard from Dr. Kowalski last week."

He was surprised at the change in subject. Furthermore, he wasn't sure at her attitude. Would she be upset that he'd emailed the professor about her?

"Oh?" he said, trying to keep his voice neutral.

"Yes," said Amanda. She matched his neutral tone but her eyes twinkled. "She told me you'd written to her that I was here. She wanted to know what I'd been doing since med school. How I ended up at the Weisman Trust."

Daniel observed her features carefully. "And did you tell her?"

"Yes, I did." She bit her lip. "The night after I told you why I quit, I went home and wrote her everything. Steven, the ICU, why I left medicine." She lifted her eyes up to his. "I figured she'd understand."

"And did she?"

She nodded, looking thoughtful. "Of course. I don't know what I was worried about." She frowned. "But she had more to say than that. She said I couldn't let fear keep me from living my life. Whatever life I want, that is."

She took a step closer to him, and he was surprised to see a different sort of expression in her eyes. She suddenly looked vulnerable and unsure.

"Do you think I'm letting fear run my life?" she asked quietly.

He wanted to reassure her, but for some reason he couldn't make his mouth work.

They stood there, both watchful, neither speaking.

Finally, Amanda smiled, and it seemed to break the tension. "That was really wonderful today," she said, changing the subject yet again. "It's impressive what you've done to meet the different needs of your patients. Just working with what you have, you've really accomplished a lot."

Daniel swallowed. "I care about my kids. They're why I do this."

"I know," said Amanda. "That is abundantly clear."

She grinned suddenly at him.

"What?" he asked.

"I just noticed. You've got a bit of paint on you."

Daniel groaned. "I'm not surprised. I thought I felt Bobby McCrae get me with his paintbrush." He looked straight at Amanda. "Where is it?"

She slowly reached out her hand to touch him lightly on the left temple. "Right there," she said, quiet now.

Daniel couldn't help himself. He reached up with his hand and closed it around hers.

They both stood frozen for a moment. Daniel found himself unable to look away, his eyes dropping to her lips. Finally, Amanda took a deliberate step towards him, closing the last small gap of space that was left between them. His free arm encircled her waist. She lifted her head to his.

Daniel was seconds from answering her invitation when they were startled by the bell of the front door.

Amanda stepped back suddenly and gave a shaky smile. "Sounds like a visitor."

Daniel nodded soberly and turned to walk back to the front of the office with Amanda following. In his head, he cursed the terrible timing that had interrupted them.

When they reached the front waiting room, however, he couldn't keep up his anger. Rita was standing there with Millie.

"Oh, good, you're both still here," Millie said. "Rita wanted to give you her picture from today."

Rita stepped forward. "This is for her," she said, pointing at Amanda. "I m-made it for you," she said, handing Amanda her creation.

Daniel saw Amanda's eyes soften. "This is lovely, Rita. Thank you!" She stooped to give the little girl a hug and then straightened. She turned the picture around so that Daniel could see it.

The man in the picture might have orange hair, and the woman purple skin, but he could plainly see that it was a painting of the two of them. They were holding hands, surrounded by kittens and one incredibly large mama cat.

"It's to say thank you," added Millie.

"I will treasure it," said Amanda. "It's going to go right up in my hotel room." She cleared her throat. "Actually, since it looks like we're done cleaning here, I think I'll probably head back to my room now." She glanced at Daniel. "Unless you need anything else?"

"Um, no," he stammered. "Thank you for your assistance."

"Anytime," she answered brightly. Almost too brightly.

She was definitely escaping.

And all he could do was watch as she latched on to Millie and Rita and left the office with them.

He shook his head, thinking of her abrupt change over the course of only a few minutes.

He couldn't speak for her, but he knew something had changed for him. He was falling for her – he'd *been* falling for her – and denying it wasn't going to work any longer.

For Daniel, only one question remained.

What was he going to do about it?

CHAPTER 7

Amanda pumped her legs as she crossed the street with Millie. Rita zipped down one of the slides and then ran on ahead to dart into the diner.

"What's the hurry?" asked Millie, scurrying alongside Amanda.

"Oh, you know," said Amanda vaguely. "I'm tired."

"Sure, everyone wants to speed-walk when they're tired."

Amanda didn't answer, but she sensed Millie glancing at her out of the corner of her eye.

"So…" said Millie, "Are you going to tell me what's going on or am I going to have to pump you for info?"

Amanda tried to give a carefree laugh, but it came off sounding nervous. She cleared her throat and tried again. "What are you talking about?" There, that sounded better.

"Oh, come on, girl," said Millie. "I am not blind or stupid. What's going on with you and Dr. Shane? I know we just interrupted *something*, and I'm dying to know what."

Amanda didn't know how to answer. Instead, she turned a set of panicked eyes toward Millie.

"Oh, honey," said Millie. "Your face is a cry for help if I ever saw one. Come with me."

Millie grabbed her arm and steered her away from the inn and into the diner.

On her way across the room, Amanda spotted Rita at the counter, where one of the waitresses was serving her chicken fingers and fries.

"Thanks, Laura!" Millie called to the waitress. "And don't let her have dessert unless she finishes her meal." The waitress waved her arm in reply as Millie led Amanda to a corner booth. It had higher sides and therefore more privacy than most of the surrounding tables.

"Sit," she ordered and Amanda weakly obeyed, happy to hide herself away. She carefully set Rita's painting on the seat beside her.

"I'm getting us shakes," continued Millie, "and then we are going to talk."

She bustled off, and Amanda dropped her head straight onto the table. She groaned.

Part of her wanted to run out of that diner and straight back across the street into Daniel's arms. The part that desperately wanted the kiss that had been about to happen. But at least some part of her remembered that it was a bad idea, and so she stayed put.

"Here," said Millie, setting a glass beside her. "Milkshakes always make me feel better."

Amanda lifted her head and took a sip. It was tasty, but it was going to take more than dessert to make this problem disappear.

Millie eyed her, allowing her a moment to enjoy her drink. But a moment was all.

"Ok, lay it on me," she commanded. "What happened?"

Haltingly, Amanda gave an abridged version of what had happened in the supply closet. Millie's eyes widened as the story went on.

"Oh. My. Gosh," she breathed when Amanda finished. "That is so romantic." She leaned forward. "You have me permission to smack me in the face for coming in when we did and blowing the whole thing."

Amanda shook her head. "No. You don't understand. I'm so grateful you came in. This thing, between Daniel and me, it can't happen."

"What?" Millie looked outraged. "Why not?"

"It is 'strongly discouraged' in my job, for one thing," said Millie. "I have to maintain some professional distance with Trust grantees. If word got out that I was involved with Daniel, there's no way he'd get the grant. There'd be too much suspicion that I was allowing my personal feelings to influence my recommendation."

"And without the grant?" asked Millie.

"Then no new medical center, no new services for the people of Highland Canyon, so speech therapy for Rita, no care close to home for Daniel's nephew, Ethan."

"Yikes," said Millie. "That is bad."

"That's not the half of it," said Amanda. "I'd also almost for sure lose my job. My boss is very strict on the no-dating rules. If Beth found out…" She shook her head. "She'd lose it."

Millie frowned. "That is a pickle." She stirred her drink with her straw. "But Amanda, putting all that aside for the moment, what about love? Doesn't that matter, too?"

Amanda laughed. "Love? I think that might be skipping ahead too fast. I'm sure I'm just one of many girls that Daniel has kissed. Well, almost kissed."

"I don't think so," said Millie. "This town isn't that big, and there aren't many secrets. I've never heard of Dr. Shane dating anyone seriously. He's always too busy with his practice."

Amanda didn't know what to say to that.

"And," Millie went on, "I can say for sure that I've never seen him look at anyone the way he does at you."

"He doesn't look at me any special way."

Millie scoffed. "He most certainly does. Like he could melt butter with just his gaze."

Amanda had to laugh at that. "Well he's not melting me."

Millie raised an eyebrow. "I don't believe you. I've seen some pretty steamy looks coming back from you, too."

Amanda closed her eyes and groaned. "Come on out and tell me. Has everyone noticed? Are we this week's gossip?"

"No, no," said Millie patting her hand. "Not everyone. I mean, me, sure. And Sarah Shane. And Kyle. And Ernie, of course."

"Even Ernie?" cried Amanda.

Millie nodded. "I'm afraid so. He saw Daniel picking you up the other night in his truck. He said it looked like a date."

"It wasn't a date," said Amanda reflexively.

Millie only continued to pat her hand, and Amanda had a suspicion that she wasn't convinced.

"What am I going to do?" asked Amanda, finally.

"Can you avoid him?"

"While I work in his office?"

"Any way of getting out of that?"

"Not without quitting my job."

"Ok, that's a no-go."

They say in silence for a moment, then Millie's eyes lit up.

"I have an idea!"

Amanda felt a jolt of hope. "What?"

"First, you go back over there right now. Find Dr. Shane and sit him down."

"Ok," said Amanda slowly. "And then?"

Millie grinned. "Then kiss him so hard that his teeth rattle."

Amanda balled up a napkin and threw it at Millie's laughing face, but she couldn't stop herself from joining in the laughter as well.

Millie wiped her eyes as they calmed down. "Honestly, I don't know what to tell you. I get all your reasons, I really do." She sighed. "But I also know I'd do almost anything to get back some time with my husband. Love is precious, and it doesn't come around often. I hate to see you ignoring a chance at it."

Amanda sobered. With Millie's youthful looks and bubbly personality, it was easy to forget that she knew her fair share of heartache. "How long were you married?"

"Three years." Amanda gave a half smile. "Much too short. But I'm very grateful to God for the time we did have together and for my sweet Rita. She reminds me of him every day."

Amanda leaned back in the booth and toyed with the rest of her shake. Was Millie right? Should she be open to the chance of love? Was that even what this was? How could she know?

She felt that, whatever path she chose, she had to be sure of herself. The stakes were just too high.

DANIEL PICKED up his phone yet again that evening. He'd tried to make himself dial Amanda four times, only to stop just before hitting her number in his phone. Now, for the fifth time, he did it again. He threw his phone down on his desk in disgust.

He was in his office, working late as he usually did on Saturdays. But tonight, he'd gotten very little accomplished. Instead, he went back and forth on this internal tug-of-war, all to make a simple phone call to a colleague.

Except Daniel knew it wasn't that simple at all.

He thought back to that morning, replaying it once again in his mind. When she'd walked into art day, it was as if the chaotic room stood still. He felt like the entire day had been elevated from a fun day with his patients to something higher, to something sacred. And then, later, holding her in his arms, even if only for a brief moment, how right she'd felt. How close he'd come to putting his lips on hers.

He startled as the ringer on his phone went off.

He checked the ID. Kyle. He pressed ignore. He didn't feel like talking to his happily married brother right that moment, with his beautiful children and happy home. He knew he was being ungenerous, but he was far too grumpy to care.

Besides, he knew why he was calling. When Daniel had first mentioned the idea of inviting Amanda to go to church with them, Kyle had jumped on the idea, almost to a weird degree. He said it was a good way to welcome her, but Daniel had noticed that Kyle had never been overly zealous about welcoming anyone else before.

Still, it suited Daniel just fine to bring Amanda to church.

But that was before the supply closet happened. What would have been a simple invitation had become much more complicated.

Now, Daniel knew he was calling to see if his brother had issued the invitation.

The phone buzzed again. Kyle.

Hitting ignore one more time, Daniel gave himself a pep talk.

"Time to man up," he said out loud. "Make the call, Daniel."

Amanda answered on the second ring.

Daniel tried to figure out from her tone if she sounded any different, but he couldn't pick up on any change. Was it possible that morning had meant nothing to her?

"Hey," he said. "I was calling to see if you were busy tomorrow. I, uh, that is, my brother and Sarah and I, we were wondering if you'd like to come to church with us. We actually attend right down the road from where you're staying."

She was silent for a moment, and he wondered what was going through her mind.

"Yes, that sounds nice," she said after a pause. "Thanks for asking."

"Good," said Daniel, feeling relieved. Whatever she'd meant that morning by running away with Millie, at least she wasn't planning to avoid him completely. "Can I come by and pick you up? So it's easy to find each other in the morning?" he hastily added.

"Sure," she said.

They worked out a time before hanging up. He sat at his desk for a moment with a goofy grin on his face.

Sure, he had no idea how she felt, but this was progress.

His phone rang.

"Hi, Kyle," he said, kicking his feet up. "You can lay off me now. Yes, she's coming tomorrow."

DANIEL PULLED his truck in front of the hotel to find Amanda once again ready and waiting in the lobby.

"You've got to be one of the most punctual people I've ever met," he said with a laugh as she walked toward him.

"Being late is unprofessional," Amanda said, but there was a twinkle in her eye.

She certainly didn't look professional this morning. She looked soft and inviting, with her simple dress and hair pulled back in a messy braid. He felt a surge of protectiveness come over him that he struggled to tamp back down.

"I thought we'd walk," he said, gesturing down the street.

"Sounds heavenly," she said. "It's a beautiful morning today."

Daniel nodded absently. "Beautiful."

They strolled in silence. Daniel wondered if he should bring up the day before. They were both adults. Perhaps it would be better to just have a frank discussion about it.

He glanced at her quickly. He wouldn't exactly say that she looked serene, but she at least seemed more at peace than all the emotions churning inside of him.

Well, if she wanted go on as if nothing had happened, then he would. And maybe it was for the best. He knew he had feelings for her, but he still didn't know how to reconcile that with the fact that she was his grant officer. He couldn't sacrifice the entire new clinic, and all the people who were depending on it, just for his emotions.

Plus, he had no idea what her feelings were. Maybe she saw the day before as one big mistake. The last thing he wanted to do was scare her away by pressing her on it.

So he started to talk, pointing out businesses and landmarks as they passed them. She asked intelligent questions along the way, exactly as he'd come to expect from her. He found himself relaxing more with every minute.

As they neared the church, they started to pass other churchgoers. Many said hello to Daniel as they met, eyeing Amanda with curiosity. Some even knew Amanda as well, and she greeted them with a friendly wave. A few were patients, but others he wasn't sure how she had met them. Perhaps all the time she spent at the diner? He shook his head, watching her. What a change from the reserved woman who would hardly speak to patients a couple short weeks ago. It seemed as if she were taking Dr. Kowalski's advice to heart and not letting fear dictate her life.

He led her inside the church, his hand unconsciously resting on the small of her back.

"There's Kyle and Sarah," he said quietly, seeing them sitting up ahead with the babies on their laps.

Amanda nodded and led the way down the aisle to join them in their pew. When his brother and sister-in-law spotted them, Daniel saw both of their faces light up. He rolled his eyes, wishing they could be subtler. He wasn't stupid – he realized they were pushing this thing between Amanda and him for whatever reason. But he wished they'd be less obvious. It was like they were convinced Daniel was on his way to dying alone unless they did something about it.

Sarah stood, and, shifting Robert to her hip, reached out to hug Amanda. When she pulled back afterwards, Daniel could see that Amanda wore the sweetest smile on her face, clearly pleased with the warm welcome. Ok, maybe he didn't mind his family being so enthusiastic if it brought such joy to Amanda's eyes.

They settled themselves into the pew, and Robert immediately climbed into Amanda's lap. Daniel watched her play quietly with him. She didn't seem to mind at all when Robert pulled a strand of hair out of her braid. Amanda simply laughed quietly and tucked the errant piece of hair behind her ear.

Daniel's eyes followed her every movement. He just couldn't help himself. She seemed so relaxed and natural. He could only hope that she truly felt as at home as she looked.

When services began, Daniel held the hymnbook for them to share so that Amanda could keep holding Robert. Ethan was fast asleep on Kyle's shoulder as usual, but Robert was typically a handful of trouble during church. Today he seemed content though with Amanda. As she sang, he reached out and patted her cheeks. Amanda looked laughingly up at Daniel, a baby hand on each side of her mouth, and Daniel's voice caught in his throat. He flushed, hoping no one had noticed as he joined back in with the singing.

When they were all seated again for the sermon, Robert crawled back over into his mother's lap, where he snuggled into her arms.

Daniel felt rather than saw Amanda relax into the pew, settling only a hair away from his shoulder. Her hand lay by her side, ending up just beside his, back to back.

He couldn't explain what happened next. It was as if there was an electric field between their hands. They weren't touching, but he could feel her. A tiny movement of her fingers, an acceptance by him, and suddenly their fingers were intertwined. Daniel was afraid to break the spell, but he couldn't help it. He turned to look down as her. She looked back up at him and locked eyes, only for a moment, before turning back to the pastor, but that moment was enough for Daniel to know. Yesterday hadn't been a mistake. She felt this connection, too.

Daniel's nerves were on edge. He wanted to jump up and cheer, or to take Amanda in his arms like she'd been the day before. But instead, he forced himself to turn his attention back to the service. Gradually, his heartbeat slowed down, and the excitement he felt transformed itself into deeper, calmer sense of joy.

Before that morning, there was a little part of him that worried that having Amanda at church with him would be a distraction. He was well aware that he hadn't made much time for God in the past couple of years – he'd just been too busy – so he didn't want to jeopardize the one time of the week when he really tried to sit in His presence.

But it turned out that having Amanda beside him grounded him in a way that he hadn't expected. It was like two parts of him had come together and made him stronger. As he attended to the pastor's words that day, they penetrated his brain in a way they hadn't in years.

And as he listened, he started to feel an inner leading, a call to embrace a new way of life, if he could only find the courage to do it.

AFTER CHURCH, Amanda stood in a group of women as they enjoyed a spread of doughnuts and coffee from the diner in a nearby reception room. The twin boys were nearby, Ethan toddling and Robert dashing to and fro, while the ladies looked on.

Though she was flanked by Sarah on one side and Millie on the other, Amanda couldn't help feeling like an outsider. The group was discussing some weather changes that had affected the ranching community, a conversation that Amanda was having trouble following, both because of her lack of familiarity with the subject and because her mind kept going back to Daniel.

Amanda thought back over the past hour. She and Daniel had released each others' hands at the end of the sermon, before everyone stood back up to sing. They'd grinned sheepishly at each other before opening the hymnal, like they were a couple of kids who'd held hands on a class field trip.

But watching him across the room now, Amanda knew she wasn't dealing with a kid. Daniel was something else entirely.

It was interesting, she thought, how different Daniel really was. Amanda had been around doctors for years. Many were dedicated to their patients, just as he was.

But in Daniel, Amanda sensed something more. He seemed to go a step beyond the usual in how much he cared and how much he was willing to sacrifice for the good of others. What made the difference? And was that what was responsible for this attraction that she couldn't help but feel?

Amanda felt someone's eyes on her and turned to see Millie watching her watch Daniel. Millie wiggled her eyebrows teasingly, and Amanda had to cover a laugh by taking a sip of her coffee.

A few minutes later, the group broke up. Millie ran off to replenish the doughnuts, and the other women drifted away to gather their children. Amanda was left standing alone with Sarah.

Sarah sighed. "Want to sit down with me? This is the only chance I'll get all day. The boys never seem to want to nap at the same time anymore."

"Sure," said Amanda, leading the way to a couple of chairs where they could still watch Robert and Ethan.

The two women settled in, Amanda balancing her empty doughnut plate on her lap.

"I'm so glad you could come today," said Sarah.

"Thanks," said Amanda. "Me too. I really enjoyed the sermon."

"Yes, Pastor Michaels usually does a wonderful job. We're lucky to have him full time in such a small town." She took a sip of her drink. "I think Daniel is pleased that you were here, too."

Amanda didn't respond to that, but instead watched Daniel where he stood talking with a group of men she didn't know. "He seems happy to be here himself," she observed.

Sarah nodded. "You're right about that. Daniel doesn't take much time off. He hasn't since Ethan was on the way."

Amanda looked questioningly at the other woman.

Sarah explained. "Daniel's always been incredibly dedicated to his job. But when we first found out that Ethan had Down syndrome, he seemed to hit an entirely new level."

She smiled, remembering. "He was so helpful to us in those early days. He sat us down and talked through all the issues we'd need to be aware of with a baby with the condition. He went really slowly, like he was afraid of scaring us, but we both found it so helpful. There wasn't anything coming that we couldn't handle with God's help, and we knew that Ethan was going to have such an advocate in Daniel.

"It was right about that time that he started talking about his great new idea – a state-of-the-art medical center right here in Highland Canyon. Something to serve the needs of our community and all the other small forgotten towns in this area. Honestly, Kyle and I thought he was dreaming too big. We didn't see how it could ever happen. But we were wrong. He found a way, as we should have known he would." She laughed. "I remember the day he found out that he was on the shortlist for a grant from the Weisman Trust. He was so happy. He actually did take off work that night." She took another sip of coffee. "He bought everyone's dinner at Millie's that evening."

"The whole place?" asked Amanda.

Sarah nodded. "It was the happiest I'd ever seen him." She looked at Amanda speculatively. "Until recently, that is."

Amanda shifted uncomfortably. "I'm not going to pretend to misunderstand you –"

"Good," said Sarah, with a mischievous expression. "That'll save time."

"But I will say," Amanda went on, "that there's really nothing going on between us." She took a deep breath. "And there can't be anyway. It would jeopardize the grant. And my career."

Sarah patted her hand. "I understand that. I really do. I've just found that sometimes God has a way of making all things possible."

Amanda wished she could be as sure about the whole situation as Sarah was. Did she even want to be with Daniel?

But then she looked across the room at him. He was standing with Ernie. The old rancher was talking, and Daniel was listening with an attitude of such respect.

Yes, she finally admitted, almost surprising herself. She did want to be with him. He was a kind, intelligent man of faith who set her pulse racing. How was she supposed to resist that? But another part of her also wanted her job, wanted her promotion. And she didn't see how she could possibly have it all.

"Have you ever thought about going back to active medicine?" Sarah asked suddenly, almost as if she were reading Amanda's thoughts.

"No," said Amanda, but then reflected that this wasn't totally true. The past week in Daniel's office really hadn't been so bad. Could she go back to working with patients? Could she open up her heart again to clinical work?

Then she remembered an image of her patient, Steven, hooked up to monitors in his ICU bed.

No, she thought. *I can't go back.*

"I'm staying at the Trust," she said. "It's a great career." She knew she sounded as if she was convincing herself, but there was nothing she could do about it. "I can do a lot of good there."

"I'm sure you can," said Sarah gently.

Amanda watched as Ethan crawled over towards them. He planted his hands and feet on the ground and stuck his bottom in the air, peeking at the two women through his feet. Amanda smiled and clapped for him, right as Robert came running over. He kept going at top speed and barreled into his brother. Ethan fell over sideways, and Robert slid over his brother's back headfirst. Both boys came up crying.

Amanda and Sarah jumped into action, each swooping down to hold and comfort a baby.

"Poor things," said Sarah, over the crying. She started to laugh, and Amanda looked at her in surprise.

"Take it to heart boys," continued Sarah over the noise. "Sometimes you're minding your own business when life charges in and knocks you down. If this isn't a life lesson, I don't know what is."

Amanda joined in her laughter.

"We can't take you guys anywhere," said Kyle from above them.

"Oh, stop that," said Sarah, "and help us up."

He reached down and pulled the baby out of Amanda's arms then helped both the women to their feet. He tried to shush the babies, but the boys were having none of it.

"Come on, sweetheart," he said to Sarah. "I think this is a sign it's time to go." He turned to Amanda. "Thanks for your help with the boys, Amanda. I hope you'll come back next Sunday."

"Let's plan for dinner later this week, ok?" added Sarah.

Amanda nodded and waved them out. The room felt especially quiet after they left, and she realized that many of the attendees had left.

Daniel was finishing up his conversation with Ernie. She watched as the two men shook hands, and then Daniel turned and found his way over to her.

He smiled, and Amanda self-consciously smoothed her hair.

"Have a good time?" he asked once he reached her.

"I did. You?"

"Yes," he said, looking at her seriously. "I know you're not supposed to go to church just for what you get out of it, but I admit, I was really moved by the sermon today."

"I don't think it's a crime to get something out of church," said Amanda with a smile. "What about the sermon struck you?"

Daniel grabbed her hand and tucked it neatly in his arm as he led her out of the room. Amanda felt a glow of pleasure at the protective way he walked with her.

"It was everything that he said about letting God work alongside you. Or rather, letting yourself work alongside God." He spoke thoughtfully. "It was a good reminder for me." He led her outside the building, and Amanda blinked in the sunlight. Daniel immediately shifted so that Amanda's eyes were shielded by the sun, and she smiled her thanks.

"As you so eloquently told me the other night," he went on as they walked down the street, "I don't have to do everything alone. I think I need that reminder sometimes. Or even a lot."

Amanda listened, glad to hear that he'd understood what she'd tried to impress upon him. She uttered a small prayer, thanking the Lord for opening Daniel's eyes to his truth.

"Does this mean you're going to stop working so late?" she teased when she was done.

"Don't get crazy," he answered in the same tone. "There's still a ton to do." He took a deep breath. "But maybe I don't have to do it all alone."

"You have me," said Amanda tentatively.

He grinned down at her. "I do, huh?"

Amanda blushed. "I mean, you have me as a representative of the Weisman Trust. Who is obviously a partner in your plans."

"Of course," said Daniel. "I figured that was what you meant."

They'd reached her hotel. Daniel turned and faced her. "Come out for lunch with me."

"Oh," said Amanda, surprised. "You're not going back in to work?"

"I'm taking the day off," he said. "How about a picnic? I'd love to show you some of the sights around here."

Amanda was taken off guard by his earnest tone, so she spoke without fully considering the implications of her acceptance.

"Ok," she said with a smile. "Give me a minute to change?"

Daniel grinned. "Sure. You run upstairs and do what you need to do. I'll go next door and get us some food to go."

"Ok," she said again. She gave a small, awkward wave and turned to go inside the Inn. She glanced over her shoulder once, sure that she would see him still standing there.

And she was right. He stood right where she'd left him, watching her go.

She felt a little shiver of anticipation for the afternoon to come.

CHAPTER 8

Daniel steered around a rut in the dirt road, careful not to jostle Amanda on the passenger seat. She was looking out the window.

"I think I'm experiencing PTSD," she said. "I vividly remember driving up and down this area trying to find my way from the airport."

"Thank goodness you persevered," he said, enjoying the way the sunlight lit up her features. "I thought I was going to have to set up a search party to find you."

"That would have been an embarrassing way to make my entrance," said Amanda. "Nothing inspires trust like being unable to follow a simple map."

"I don't know about simple," said Daniel. "This is a wild area. Not everything is marked as clearly as it could be."

"I'm glad you know where you're going," she said. "Speaking of which, where are we going?"

"Patience, doctor," he said. "You'll see when we get there. We're not too far now."

Amanda pulled her feet up onto the seat in a cross-legged position. She'd changed into jeans, a light fleece, and tennis shoes, and it was the first time Daniel had seen her so casually dressed. Well, other than that night she was in her pajamas on his front porch, a moment he'd replayed in his mind more than once.

He found he rather liked her relaxed appearance. She looked like she could fit in anywhere in the area, and no one would know she was a transplant.

They'd started the drive through some of the grasslands that surrounded the town, but they were now approaching the nearby hills. It was these hills and valleys that had spawned the name "Highland Canyon."

Amanda leaned forward to take in the view. "My parents would love it out here. They're big outdoors people."

Daniel was interested. He'd never heard her talk about her family before.

"Montana is nothing but the outdoors," he said. "Maybe they should come visit."

"Maybe," she said.

"Do they live in Seattle, too?" he asked.

"Nearby," said Amanda. "When they retired, they left the city for a bit of wilderness." She gave him an arch look. "Washington has some of that, too."

He laughed. "I'm sure it does."

Amanda sighed. "Not that I ever see it. I rarely get the chance to leave the city for a weekend. Unless I'm on a grantee trip, that is, and that could end up being anywhere."

"I'm sure your parents are happy to see you when you can make it."

Amanda nodded. "Sure. Visits were a little tense for a while, when I first gave up practicing medicine, but they came around."

"They didn't understand why you quit?" he asked.

"No." Amanda looked at Daniel. "I think in some ways, it requires someone who's been through those same struggles to understand."

Daniel reached out a hand and covered hers. He gave a reassuring squeeze before letting go and putting his hands back on the wheel. She smiled at him.

"I hope you're hungry," he said a few minutes later, as he pulled his truck to the side of the road. "We're here."

Amanda lifted the picnic basket he'd packed from the seat between them and then jumped out of the passenger door.

"Hey," called Daniel. He climbed down from the truck and came around to meet her. "Let me carry that."

Amanda meekly handed him the basket. "I could make a point about equality for women right now, but, honestly, it's pretty heavy." She gave a grin. "So I'll let you."

Daniel laughed and held out his hand for her to grab. "Come on. We're going this way."

Together they walked a couple hundred feet from the road. They were at the top of a large plateau, and Daniel walked Amanda carefully towards the edge. He knew the moment when he'd brought her to the right spot because she abruptly stopped in place.

"This is incredible," she breathed.

Daniel grinned. This was one of his favorite spots in the area. The scrub and grass-covered plateau looked out over a deep rock gully. The black of the rocks provided a striking backdrop against the stand of evergreen trees that dotted its edge. As Daniel looked at it with fresh eyes, he realized the colors reminded him of something.

When Amanda turned her awestruck green eyes on him, her black hair glinting in the sun, he realized what it was.

He shook his head, feeling momentarily dazed. "Want to sit down?" he asked.

They found a clear patch of ground and pulled out the sheet Daniel had placed in the top of the picnic basket.

Amanda spread it out. "Is this one of the linens we used when Bella had her kittens?" she asked, one eyebrow raised.

Daniel laughed. "Yes. But it's been washed."

Amanda shook her head and started unpacking the food. "Trust a doctor to bring bed sheets. Did you bring patient gowns for us to put on if it gets cold?"

"You'll be glad of those gowns when the temperature drops," he teased.

Amanda playfully rolled her eyes.

Daniel sat down on the sheet and helped Amanda with the food. "I ran into Millie in the diner, so I asked her for some pointers on what you like to eat." He cleared his throat. "Mainly she said you liked everything, so I was safe."

Amanda groaned. "Unfortunately, Millie is right. I can eat anything. And do."

"My kind of woman," said Daniel, enjoying the blush that spread across her cheeks at his words.

Amanda kneeled on the sheet and tucked her feet to one side. "Shall we pray?" she asked.

Daniel nodded, letting her take the lead. She closed her eyes to recite the blessing, but he couldn't take his eyes off of her. Since he'd met her, the initial attraction he'd felt had grown so quickly. He was a long way from the initial admiration he'd felt, and he wasn't sure when the transition began. He couldn't believe the good luck that had brought her into his life.

Or maybe not good luck, he thought, her prayer washing over him. He had a feeling that she was more like a gift from God than a lucky find.

Now if only he knew if she loved him too.

When she finished, she opened her eyes and met his gaze. She didn't seem surprised to find him watching her. She gave him a long, appraising look, as if wondering what he was going to do.

He took a deep breath to try to master his thoughts. He managed what he hoped was a nonchalant smile. "Let's eat."

AMANDA LEANED back on the ground and stretched her arms above her head.

"Another amazing Montana meal in the books," she said. She rolled onto her side and propped her head up on her hand. "I would never stop eating if I lived here all the time."

"It's a struggle," Daniel said, laying down and mirroring her position. "I almost gave up medicine for a career in competitive eating."

"You did, huh?" asked Amanda, her mouth quirking up at the corner.

"But in the end, my patients won out over eating as many pies and hot dogs and chicken wings that I wanted. But just barely."

Amanda laughed and rolled onto her back again. "Ug. I am so stuffed."

Daniel jumped up. "Only one cure for that. Let's get you moving."

He held out two hands for Amanda to grab and then pulled her to her feet.

"How are you so chipper?" she asked. "You ate more than I did."

"All that competitive eating training," he said lightly.

Amanda laughed again and allowed herself to be led away from the picnic.

While they walked, she was surprised at how happy she felt. She'd been nervous at first about coming out on this picnic. She wasn't sure what would happen to all her resolutions to keep things professional with him once they were out together.

But so far, it had been easy. Everything had been light and fun, and she was so glad she'd come.

Besides, she reasoned, even if some *small* part of her did possibly have feelings for Daniel, what did that signify? Nothing. She still knew from her own observations that he really was an excellent doctor and that he'd thought through the plan of the new clinic from every angle. She wasn't seeing him through rose-colored glasses. Her recommendation would be coming from a place of logic and reason.

But she was willing to let logic and reason slip a little bit this afternoon. The setting was truly spectacular, with that wild gorge spread out before them. She half expected to see a bear or moose come wandering through the scenery. She and Daniel walked hand-in-hand, occasionally stopping to appreciate a certain viewpoint or good-naturedly argue with one another. Amanda found herself laughing constantly. It was so easy to forget about her fear when she was out with him.

After half an hour of walking, they at last they pulled up in front of a large rock formation that protruded from the ground. Daniel leaned back onto the vertical expanse of rock and held his arm open for Amanda to join him. She slipped beside him and, after a moment's hesitation, leaned against him, glad for the chance to rest.

His arm tightened around her and she sighed. "Thank you for bringing me here, Daniel."

"My pleasure," he said, and she was surprised to hear his voice was lower than usual.

She froze, torn between enjoying the feel of his arm around her and scared of what might be coming.

"Amanda," he said after a minute in this position. "I heard what you said a couple weeks ago. The night we ate dinner with Kyle and Sarah. You said that you weren't supposed to date grantees."

Amanda nodded against his shoulder. "I thought you might have."

"I understand the reasoning behind it," Daniel went on. "And I want you to know that I don't want to jeopardize anything for you. I'm happy to stay just friends and colleagues if that's what you want."

She looked out across the idyllic view, almost afraid to look at him right then.

"But just so you know –" Daniel leaned back so that Amanda could see his face, and she was instantly fascinated by how dark his eyes had become.

"Just so you know," he said again, "'friends and colleagues' is not what I want."

Amanda felt a rush of heat at his words. She found herself unable and unwilling to stop what she knew was coming next. Sending a quick prayer up to God for what she was about to do, she took the plunge.

"Me either," she said as bravely as she could, and then did what she'd wanted to do all day. She kissed him.

If she'd expected him to be surprised into inaction, she was wrong. Daniel entered into the kiss right away as enthusiastically as if he'd started it himself.

One hand came up through her hair to cradle her head, while the other tightly gripped her waist. Her arms wrapped around his shoulders, and she let herself be momentarily carried away by the rush of feelings.

When they finally broke apart, they stood with their foreheads touching, both of them grinning widely.

"That was not very professional, Dr. Garvas," Daniel said, lightly kissing the tip of Amanda's nose.

"Professionalism is overrated," she said, burying her head into his shoulder. She felt him laugh at her words.

Daniel half-groaned, half-sighed, and held Amanda back from him, one hand on each of her arms. He took a deep breath and gave her a wry smile. "We'd better get back."

"Ok," said Amanda reluctantly. It seemed such a shame to end the beautiful afternoon, but she knew he was right. It would be getting dark soon, and, from the way she felt right now, she should probably go back to her room and cool off.

Together, they headed back down the path they'd taken. She knew they'd have trials to manage, and that the way forward wasn't perfectly clear, but Amanda hadn't felt so happy as she did right then in a long time.

As a team, the two of them packed up the remaining food, folded up the sheet, and loaded everything back into the truck.

And if they paused for a kiss or two on the way back, no one was the wiser.

DANIEL PULLED up in front of the hotel.

"Thank you for a wonderful day," said Amanda, unbuckling her seat belt.

"I was about to say the same thing," said Daniel. He leaned over and kissed her gently on the cheek. "For a wonderful, stupendous, life-changing day."

Amanda laughed. "That's pretty good."

"I call it like I see it," he said, and when Amanda turned her face to his, he stole one more kiss.

His head was so full of her that it took him a moment to realize that his pants had suddenly started ringing.

He groaned, pulling his phone out of his back pocket. "What timing," he muttered.

He checked the caller and saw his brother's name.

"Mind if I take it real quick?" he asked Amanda.

"Go ahead," she said. "I'll save your place."

Daniel grinned at her as he answered the phone. "Hi, Kyle. What's up?"

"Hey," Daniel heard, immediately noting the concern in his brother's voice. "I think we might have a problem with Ethan."

"What's going on?"

"He's asleep right now, but he's breathing so loudly. I know you told me we needed to watch out for sleep apnea. Is it possible that's what's going on?"

"Has he been congested during the day?" asked Daniel.

"A little. Sarah did say she thought he was coming down with a cold."

Daniel thought for a moment. Kids with Down syndrome were definitely at a higher risk of breathing troubles. He wouldn't feel completely comfortable until he'd seen him.

"It's probably the cold. But I'd like to check him out just in case."

"Should I bring him to the office?"

"Don't be crazy. He's asleep. I'll come to you."

Daniel could hear the relief in his brother's voice. "Thanks, man."

"Be there in a few."

As soon as he hung up, Amanda asked him, "Is everything ok?"

Daniel shook his head. "I've got to go check on Ethan and make sure he's breathing normally. Kyle and Sarah are concerned."

"Of course." She rebuckled her seat belt.

Daniel paused at her actions. "You're coming with me?" Was she actually volunteering for extra doctor work?

Amanda looked momentarily uncertain. "I mean, if that's ok."

Daniel smiled and shifted the truck into gear. "It's more than ok. Let's go."

On the way over, Amanda shared some new ideas about treatments for Down syndrome kids with Daniel that she'd read up on.

He glanced at her in surprise.

"Where did you learn all this?"

"Dr. Kowalski," she said. "We've been corresponding. After we connected, she was asking my

125

opinion on a couple of placements for her interns in Seattle. And then we got to talking about other things."

"And you asked her about Ethan?" he said, touched.

"Sure. We want to get him the best care possible, right? I knew Dr. Kowalski would have some great ideas for us."

Daniel could only nod, amazed again at her use of the words "we" and "us."

When they pulled up to his brother's house, Sarah and Kyle met them at the door.

"Thank you so much," she said, bringing them in. "Hopefully it's nothing. We were just on edge. He hasn't been feeling well today."

"You guys could have called me sooner," said Daniel.

"I know," said Sarah. "But you already do so much for us. I didn't want to bother you."

"It's never a bother," said Daniel. He opened up his portable doctor's kit he'd brought along and pulled out a stethoscope. "Let's have a listen."

Sarah led Daniel and Amanda into the baby's room. A small nightlight gave off enough of a glow to see the babies. Daniel immediately put the instrument to Ethan's chest and listened to the rise and fall of breathing. He frowned and looked at Amanda.

"I'd like a second opinion," he said and handed her the stethoscope.

Amanda listened quietly for a moment, moving the instrument to various spots of Ethan's chest. She pulled out her phone and used it as a flashlight to examine Ethan's ribs. When she was done, she motioned that they could leave the room.

Once in the hallway, they conferred with Kyle and Sarah.

"What do you think?" he asked Amanda.

She hesitated a moment, clearly thinking through her answer. "I don't think there's anything to worry about for tonight. There's no wheezing, no respiratory distress."

Daniel had come to the same conclusion. "However," he added, "I do think he's going to need a sleep study in the next year or so to make sure apnea isn't developing."

"I agree," said Amanda.

Sarah and Kyle looked relieved.

"So his breathing is fine?" asked Kyle.

Daniel nodded. "For now." He clapped a hand on his brother's shoulder. "Nothing we can't handle."

"Thank the Lord," prayed Sarah. She smiled at them. "Come into the kitchen for some tea. We really appreciate you coming out here." She tucked Amanda's arm into hers and led the way into the kitchen. Kyle followed, clearly feeling a weight lifted.

Daniel remained behind in the hallway alone. He felt as though he'd just had a mini wake-up call, reminding him of why he'd started down the road of building the new clinic in the first place. They'd been remarkably lucky with Ethan's health up until now, but how long until their luck changed? He had to get the new clinic up and running, as soon as possible.

Ethan's health depended on it.

AMANDA WOKE up the next day already grinning. She jumped out of bed and got ready in record time. She paused in front of the picture that Rita had made for her on her way out. She'd hung it on the wall the other day when she was trying to boost her spirits. Now she lightly touched Daniel's orange marker face.

"See you soon," she said.

On her way to Daniel's practice, she swung by Millie's.

"Morning, Ernie," she called. He raised his mug of coffee in her direction in recognition.

Amanda was in no mood to wait for a full breakfast, so she ordered some doughnuts to go from the waitress working the counter.

As the waitress fetched the order, Amanda saw Millie in the kitchen. As soon as they made eye contact, Millie came running out. She gripped Amanda's arm and leaned in.

"Tell me what happened," she whispered. "Dr. Shane came in here asking what you like to eat and bought half of our food, and next thing I know I see you driving off together!"

"We had a picnic," said Amanda, her eyes sparkling.

"I guessed that much," said Millie. "But what happened?"

Amanda gave a quick, abridged version of the day, but naturally included the most exciting part.

When she heard about the kiss, Millie let out a squeal that caused Ernie to jerk his head up from his newspaper.

"Sorry," called Millie, waving her hand distractedly. She turned back to her friend, and Amanda had to laugh at the expression on her face.

"I can't believe it," she said. "That's even more romantic than the supply closet."

"I should hope so," said Amanda. "We can do better than a supply closet."

Right then the waitress appeared with her bag of doughnuts. Thanking her, Amanda turned back to Millie. "I gotta go."

Millie shook her head. "I bet you do. Get on over there, girl!"

Amanda laughed and headed out the door.

Daniel was speaking with a few of his nurses when Amanda walked into the waiting room.

"Good morning," she called to everyone. "I've brought doughnuts." She opened the bag and passed it around. While everyone was busy selecting their treats, she met his gaze and gave a secret smile that he knew was just for him.

Unfortunately, patients were already coming in the door. He busied himself greeting them, gave a few last minute instructions to his nurses, and was about to head back to his office to prepare for the first appointments. He paused for a moment before leaving the busy room.

"Dr. Garvas," he asked, "would you please assist me for a minute?"

"Of course," she said and followed behind.

As soon as he closed his office door behind them, he gathered her into his arms and kissed her good morning.

"Much better," he said after a moment, when she was breathless and laughing. "Now I can start my day."

"So much better than a doughnut," said Amanda.

"Heck," he said, "I might get a doughnut, too." He held her back at arm's length. "I see you're back to Ms. Professional."

"What do you expect me to wear?" she asked with a laugh. "Jeans and a fleece? My pink jammies?"

"I liked those pink jammies," he said, pulling her to him again in a hug. "I couldn't believe it when I came onto the porch that night and you were sitting there. I think I fell for you then."

"Oh, stop," she laughed, swatting him. "We've got patients to see."

Daniel paused for a moment. "We?" he asked, hardly believing his ears.

"Well, you," said Amanda. "But I'm helping right?"

He kissed her cheek. "You bet." He finally let her go. He turned to his desk to glance at the schedule for the day. "Wow. We've got lots of kids coming in today." He looked up. "I think my receptionist got a little ahead of herself when she found out you'd be helping. We've got tons of patients."

Amanda walked by his side. "Let's get cracking then."

He stared at her. Where had this self-assured doctor come from? She never would have been so eager even a week before.

She didn't seem to notice his amazement. She gave him a quick kiss on the cheek before heading for the door. "I'll take Room One," she called over her shoulder. He could only shake his head and follow.

The day flew by in a flurry of appointments. They were so busy they scarcely had time to talk to each other unless it was about a patient.

By the end of the day, they were both tired. Everyone but them had gone home for the day, and they were enjoying a minute of peace after all the hectic activity.

As Daniel thought back over the day, two moments stood out in his mind.

The first was early in the morning. Daniel had just completed a well-check for a six-year-old boy named Carlos. Carlos was a sweet kid, but he hated shots with a passion. Whenever someone walked in with a needle, he'd scream and flail about until he literally made himself sick on the floor. His mother tried to control him, but she usually couldn't. Understandably, Daniel's nurses usually didn't want to be the unlucky person picked for shot duty.

He heard the three on-duty nurses arguing out in the hallway. He'd already finished his part of the appointment and was going on to the next room around the corner. Each nurse was trying to convince the others that someone else should go in and take care of Carlos.

Daniel was about to step in to settle the silly argument when he heard Amanda speak to the group.

"Give me the shot," she said. Daniel peaked around the corner to watch. The nurses stood in surprise as Amanda strode into the room. When they spotted Daniel watching from around the corner, they promptly split up to see to other duties.

Daniel crept up to the door of the exam room.

"Ok, Carlos," Amanda was saying, "this won't be bad at all. Just a quick stick."

Daniel saw Carlos take a deep breath to start screaming, but Amanda interrupted the boy quickly.

"Carlos," she said in a very firm voice. "I hope you are not going to yell at me for keeping you healthy. Now please pick which arm you want."

"What?" he asked.

"Which arm?" she repeated. "You get to choose."

Hesitantly, he pointed to his left arm.

"Excellent. Now I'm going to count. Should we go on two or three?"

Carlos gave her a long look. "Two," he finally said.

"Two it is." When he looked like he was going to yell again she held up her hand. "One more thing. Can you cough?"

Carlos paused. "Yeah, I can cough."

"Let me hear it."

The boy gave a small cough.

"No, no, that's not nearly big enough. Try again."

This time he coughed louder.

"Much better. Now when I say two, I want you to give a big cough. The biggest you can, ok?"

Carlos nodded.

Amanda help up the needle. "No screaming, right?"

Carlos bobbed his head again.

"Good. One, two!" Carlos coughed as instructed, and the shot was completed.

"Nice work," said Amanda warmly, placing a bandage over the injection site. "That was the best cough I've ever heard."

Carlos glowed while Amanda stood and dropped the needle in the room's sharps container.

"You're all done," she said to Carlos's mom.

She walked out of the room where she promptly ran into Daniel.

"Ouch," she said, losing her balance.

"I've got you," he said, reaching out his arms to steady her. "Amanda, that was excellent." He shook his head at her. "No one can get Carlos to do that."

Amanda cocked her head at him and smiled. "Please. I did allergy skin tests for a living. That's about 30 shots all in a row. I could totally handle one shot for Carlos." And with a sassy look, she strode off to continue her rounds.

The second standout moment of the day was later in the afternoon. Daniel's patient was a Maria, a thirteen-year-old girl whom Daniel had been treating for several years. On this appointment, however, she seemed vague about her symptoms, and she kept looking down instead of at him. Daniel was having a hard time getting to the heart of what was wrong when Maria's mother spoke up.

"Dr. Shane, am I right in thinking that you have a female doctor helping you right now?"

Daniel nodded. "Yes. Dr. Garvas is here." He paused as Maria's mother gave him a significant look. "Why don't I step out and see if she is available?"

Maria looked relieved, and her mother smiled. "Thank you, Doctor."

Daniel headed down the hallway where he found Amanda studying a patient chart.

"Hey," he said, "would you mind taking the patient in Room Four? Maria's a teenage girl, and she's requesting a female doctor."

Amanda smiled. "Sure." She closed the chart and handed it off to Daniel. "You want to take my patient in Three?"

"Deal," he said, amazed all over again as the self-assurance he saw in her.

There were nurses up and down the hall behind them, but Amanda brushed his fingers with her own unobtrusively as she walked past him.

He closed his eyes for one second to take a deep breath before heading off to see his patient.

Later he'd caught up with Amanda.

"Maria?" he asked.

"Urinary tract infection," said Amanda.

"Ah. No wonder she didn't want to talk to me," said Daniel.

Amanda nodded. "But not to worry – we got her all taken care of." She turned to walk away, but Daniel reached out to grab her hand. She stopped, pleasure written on her face.

"Thank you," he whispered.

She smiled. "You're welcome," she whispered back. "Now let go before someone sees." She gave a wicked grin before she walked away.

Over the next week, Daniel watched in wonder as Amanda blossomed. She treated a wide variety of patients, calling on him less and less often to take a case. Patients had started to recognize her and greet her as they played on the front porch and in the waiting room. She took an active interest in all the children, and she'd built up a rapport with all of the nurses.

By Thursday, Amanda looked perfectly at home in the practice. It was a particularly busy day, with tons of kids on the schedule. That evening, when the building was finally cleared out, Amanda and Daniel were able to relax in his back office. They each were reclining in a chair. Amanda had kicked her shoes off, and he was gently rubbing her feet.

"What a day," she said. "I've still got to go home and update my report."

"Are you still working on that?" asked Daniel.

"Of course. Technically, that's the point of me helping out in your office, remember? So that I can see how you run your practice and use that to inform the grant recommendation?"

Daniel rubbed her right foot gently with his thumbs. "So what are you going to write about today? Devilishly handsome doctor saves the world, one patient at a time?"

Amanda smiled. "That's sweet that you think I'm devilishly handsome," she said, and he laughed.

She sighed. "I'm really going to write about the type and number of patients we saw. How the practice was staffed today. The need in the community. Etc. Beth loves that kind of stuff." Her phone buzzed, and she picked it up from beside her.

"Speaking of. It's Beth." She glanced at Daniel. "Mind if I take this?"

"Go ahead," he said. "I'm busy anyways." He pulled on one of her toes and made her laugh.

"Hello?" said Amanda in the phone. "Hi, Beth. Yes, I know… Uh huh… We're just finishing up for the day."

Daniel watched Amanda as she talked. As he'd gotten to know her better, he'd realized that her delicate features showed every thought going through her head. He amused himself picking out when she was annoyed with something that Beth was saying. Near the end of the conversation, though, her expression changed. She looked disappointed, and, a moment later, resigned.

It looked as though Amanda was trying to finish up her conversation with Beth. "Yes, I completely understand. You know I will… Ok… Sure, Beth… I've got to run now, if that's ok… Yes, I'll definitely keep you updated…"

"What's up?" asked Daniel as Amanda finally hung up the phone.

"What do you mean?" she asked, trying and failing to look innocent.

"Come on, Amanda," he said. "I can tell she said something that threw you."

"No, it's just Beth being Beth." Amanda pulled her feet out of his hands and slipped on her shoes.

"Come on, let's get some dinner. I'm starving."

"You're always starving," Daniel teased, willing to go along with her light mood. He knew there was something Amanda wasn't telling him about the phone call, but he trusted her to tell him when the time was right.

In the meantime, he was happy to soak up every second with her that he could get.

CHAPTER 9

Amanda sat up in her hotel room, staring at her computer screen. She had a big job to complete, and she was finding it intimidating.

The evening, she hadn't been entirely honest with Daniel about Beth's phone call. Beth hadn't called only to check up on her, though Amanda knew that that motivation had definitely been part of it. She'd also requested that Amanda go ahead and submit the final grant recommendation report. She felt Amanda had stayed in Highland Canyon long enough, both to thoroughly explore the new clinic proposal and to test the new method of evaluating grantees.

Amanda had hated to tell Daniel and spoil the fun mood of the evening, so she tried to put it out of her mind through dinner. But once she was finally back in her room for the night, she couldn't put off the truth any longer.

And now she was staring at her screen.

Though she'd worked on it for weeks, Amanda wrestled with the final report. She kept agonizing over word choices and what to include, Part of the problem was that she knew how important the grant was. She felt like her entire career and certainly her promotion were riding on her doing a good job. And, what had become even more important to her, the very possibility of the new medical clinic hung upon her doing a good job. She had to convince Beth that this project was worthwhile, otherwise the new center would never happen.

And she knew that it needed to happen, sooner rather than later. She thought back to the night she and Daniel had gone out to examine Ethan. Kyle and Sarah had both seemed happy and relieved after hearing that everything was fine, which Amanda could understand. Unfortunately, she also understood the more troubled expression on Daniel's face. She'd seen it on doctor's faces many times before. He had concerns about Ethan's health that he wasn't voicing.

She thought back to her own struggles with her patient Steven. She'd started to doubt herself after he ended up in the ICU, she knew, doubts that were only compounded when she was taking care of patients whom she was especially attached to. What must Daniel be going through now, treating his own nephew?

Seeing Daniel's troubled face swimming through her mind, she knew she had to do the best job possible on this report. As a result, she didn't finish it until 3:00 in the morning. Wearily, she went it off to Beth before crawling into bed.

Despite the late hour, she lay awake for a while. Completing the grant report meant her time was coming to an end. She tried to block out of her mind what that would mean for her, hating the thought of leaving Daniel. She tried to tell herself that it would be good for her to get back to her career. Maybe her promotion would come through. The thought didn't excite her like it would have one month before, but she pushed that out of her head. This was the best thing to do for Daniel.

Finally, Amanda dropped into a fitful sleep.

The next morning, Amanda walked into the office, sipping the largest cup of coffee she could get from

Millie's. She'd had to drag herself into the office, dreading having to tell Daniel the news.

"Good morning," she called walking down the hallway, trying to fake an energy that she didn't feel.

"Hey!" said Daniel, poking his head out of his office. "You beat everybody this morning." He took one look at her face and frowned. "Are you ok?"

Amanda nodded as she walked past him into the room.

"Mind if I sit down?" she asked. "I'm still half asleep. I had some trouble going to bed last night."

"I'm sorry," said Daniel. "You should have slept in. I can handle it here."

"I wanted to talk to you before the staff showed up." She took one more sip of coffee for courage and then launched in.

"I submitted my final grant recommendation last night," she said. "The report will go to Beth, who has the final say on whether it goes to the Board of Directors. But I was very clear that I give the project my full support. I think the new medical center is an excellent investment and will serve the needs of many people in this region."

Daniel listened to her with a smile slowly widening across his face. "That's wonderful news!" he said, kneeling in front of her and grasping her hands. "Whew. I thought it was something bad. You looked so grim."

Amanda tried to smile and continued to explain. "Now, I should warn you that Beth is a big micromanager – I think I always have expected her to show up in town one day to check up on me – so she may have some follow-up questions for me to look into before she'll take it to the Board. But we'll see." She took another sip. "Maybe she's learning to trust me."

Daniel stared into her eyes. "Thank you," he said seriously. "Your help on this has been the greatest gift. I never could have done it without you."

"Surely not," said Amanda, with a little laugh. "Aren't you the doctor who does it all by himself?"

"Not anymore," he said and rose from his knees to put his arms around her.

Amanda allowed herself to relax in his hug for just a moment before pulling back.

She pushed a strand of hair behind her ear and looked down at her lap. "Well, there is one consequence that we haven't discussed yet."

"What's that?"

"Once I've submitted my report, there's no more reason for me to stay here," she said quietly.

Daniel sat back on his feet. "Oh." He looked stunned. "I guess I should have thought of that."

Amanda continued to talk to fill the silence. "In my email, I asked Beth for permission to stay slightly longer to help with your caseload. I know they scheduled more patients than normal since I was here, and I'd hate to leave you with double patients." She took a deep breath. "Still, another week is probably all I have. I'll have to go back."

After a moment, Daniel spoke slowly, cautiously. "And you want to go back?"

Amanda opened her mouth to reply, but suddenly found unsure of how to answer.

What if she did stay in Highland Canyon? Maybe she and Daniel had a future together here. She sensed that what was growing between them was something strong.

But what would she do here? She hated to admit it, but she was still too scared to go back to practicing medicine full time. She couldn't bear it if something went wrong with one of her patients. And besides, she had a great job waiting for her in Seattle, maybe even a promotion. If she went back, she could keep helping people through her grant work.

Faintly, Amanda started hearing sounds that others were joining them for a day of work. She grabbed onto the lifeline from her confused thoughts and avoided Daniel's question entirely.

"We'd better get going," she said, standing up. She held out a hand to help Daniel to his feet. "Patients will be checking in soon."

She hurried out the door, away from the question that Daniel still held in his eyes.

DANIEL WENT for a walk to clear his mind after the last patient left that evening. Amanda had dashed out the door as soon as they closed up for the day, pausing only to share that Beth had approved her request to stay for one more week before she ran off to the diner.

Daniel didn't try to stop her. He was starting to recognize her escape pattern now. She liked to run when things got intense.

He'd been floored by the news that she'd be gone in a week. In the back of his mind, he must have known that the current state of things couldn't last, but he'd managed to block it from his thoughts pretty thoroughly. But suddenly, a future without Amanda was looming in front of him.

He hated the thought of not having her here with him. To go to church with him. To go on weekend adventures. To share his busy days. To catch up over dinner. Even his beloved pediatric practice, that he'd built from the ground up alone – he didn't want without her in it.

He wanted her in his life.

But could he make her want to stay?

He thought through what she'd said that morning. One week. That was all she had left. It wasn't much time to change her mind if she was intent on going. But something in her conflicted expression that morning told him that she wasn't quite sure what she wanted.

Without him consciously realizing it, his steps took him toward the church. When he noticed where he was, he spotted a paper sign taped to the door.

"Men's Bible Study, 6:30 pm," he read out loud. With a stab of guilt, Daniel realized this was the study group that his pastor kept inviting him to. He'd ignored the invitation each time, always feeling that he was too busy.

Pausing at the door, Daniel checked his watch. It was only 6:10. He could go in if he wanted to. He felt a little awkward about it, though. Outside of Sunday services, he hadn't been inside the building for ages.

He wondered uncomfortably if he'd been taking God for granted. Had he been consumed with work, when maybe he should have made more time for his Lord?

"Well," said a voice behind him, "are you going in or not?"

Daniel turned to see Ernie on the street behind him.

"That's what I'm trying to figure out," said Daniel.

Ernie nodded slowly. "Been there myself." He inclined his head to the side. "Walk with me, son. I'm going to see about a horse."

Why not? Daniel thought. He had time either way. Daniel turned from the church door and fell in step besides the older man. In his button-down shirt and khakis, he felt ridiculously cosmopolitan compared to Ernie, who looked as if he'd stepped right out of a cowboy movie.

The two men walked quietly for a moment. Daniel knew that Ernie had never been a big talker, and his own thoughts were too busy to admit for much speech.

Ernie led the way down the street to the side of a wide field that was fenced in by rough wooden planks. There were ten or so horses in the field, swatting their tails and grazing in the grass.

Ernie leaned against the fence, motioning for Daniel to join him.

"Thinking about buying that one," he said, pointing to a white and grey stallion that was standing apart from the group. It was an especially tall horse with almost a regal bearing.

"He's a stubborn one, though," continued Ernie. "Always wants to go his own way, on his own. Doesn't like taking direction from people." He turned a slow eye on Daniel. "But he's majestic, isn't he?"

Daniel bowed his head in agreement. The horse was truly beautiful with its distinctive coloring. Though it was still, Daniel could sense the latent energy coming off of it.

Ernie gave a deep sigh. "Figure if I can just get him to learn to depend on me a little bit, trust me even, he might be a great addition. But can he change?"

Ernie turned a sharp eye on Daniel. "What do you think?" he asked gruffly. "Can he change?"

Daniel swallowed, holding the rancher's gaze. "I sure hope so."

Ernie turned back to the field. "I do, too."

The two men stood in silence for a few minutes. Finally, Ernie spoke without turning to look at Daniel.

"'Reckon you've got somewhere you need to go."

Daniel nodded. He did. Clapping his friend on the back, he turned to go. With a renewed sense of purpose, he strode back to the church, pulled open the door, and passed inside.

It was time to bring his troubles to God.

AMANDA TRIED the front door of Daniel's practice. Locked. She knocked loudly, guessing that maybe he was in the back. No answer.

She'd only been gone from the practice for half an hour when she realized that she shouldn't have run out on him. Whatever their relationship was, it deserved more than her avoiding him anytime conflicts arose. But when she returned to talk to him, she found that he'd already left for the day.

Absentmindedly, she sat down on the porch swing and pushed back. Just what exactly was their relationship? They'd really only been romantically involved for a short time. Why did it feel like so much longer than that? What was the source of their connection?

She dropped her head onto her hands.

Lord, is he the one for me? Is this really what you want from me?

"And if so," she whispered aloud, "why do I feel so afraid?"

"Amanda?" called a soft voice. Amanda looked up in surprise and found Sarah watching her from the bottom of the stairs.

"Hi," she said, looking at Amanda in concern. "Is everything ok?"

Amanda gave a desperate laugh. "No, not really."

Sarah climbed the steps. "Mind if I join you?"

Amanda scooted over. "Not at all."

Sarah settled back, her expression peaceful.

"Where are the boys?" asked Amanda.

"Kyle's got them. It was kind of a long day. I think Robert is teething, and Ethan refused to eat most of the day, and then I got stung by a wasp!" She held out an arm to show a red welt to Amanda.

"That is a tough day," said Amanda.

Sarah laughed. "Kyle came home and took one look at me and told me to take a break. So I went for a drive, but when I passed you sitting up here, though, I thought I'd better check on you."

"Always taking care of someone," said Amanda.

Sarah chuckled. "It's hard to turn off the mothering instinct."

The women rocked back and forth. The light was just starting to fade, and Amanda could see hints of sunset to the west. She remembered her first night in Montana, stuck out on that highway, watching sunset fall. That night, she couldn't have imagined where she'd end up.

"Where's Daniel?" asked Sarah.

"I don't know," said Amanda. "I, uh… Well, I kind of ran out on him this afternoon. I came back to apologize, but he's missing."

"You ran out on him?" asked Sarah.

Amanda nodded. "Like literally." She whooshed her hands, one past the other. "Ran right out the door."

Sarah laughed. "He'll be back. He can never stay away from work for long."

"I know." Amanda looked at Sarah. "You must be really excited about possibly getting a new medical clinic. It would be such a help for Ethan."

"I am," said Sarah. "We've prayed and prayed for God to show us the way to properly care for Ethan as he grows older, and I think we've found it in the new clinic. It will be a relief once it's a reality." She looked at Amanda. "We're very grateful for the work you've done." Amanda shrugged nonchalantly, but Sarah pressed on. "Really, we are. The whole town is. Everyone has felt the lack of medical facilities in some way or another. You've helped a lot of people through your time here."

"Thank you," said Amanda, shifting in her seat. "But it's a really great investment from the point of view of the Weisman Trust. We're all about advancing healthcare. The new clinic is going to be great for the whole region. It's not often that rural areas have access to good facilities." She shifted in her seat. "It's something I noticed in med school. Most of the placements for internships are in cities. But that doesn't really train you for the reality of practicing in the country. I mean, I delivered a litter of kittens on my second day here! That wasn't covered in my training."

"I bet," said Sarah.

"And then if all the student internships are in cities, the students are more likely to take jobs in cities when they graduate, because it's what they know. And then, with more of the talent in cities, more of the internships end up in cities, and on and on. It's a self-perpetuating cycle."

Amanda suddenly felt like she was getting carried away and stopped. But Sarah appeared to still be listening interestedly.

Amanda gave a small self-conscious laugh. "All of this is to say that this is a good investment for us, too. So no need for the thanks."

"You're so passionate about your work," said Sarah.

Amanda thought about it. "I suppose I am. It gave me a way to channel my interests when I quit practicing myself."

"Why did you stop treating patients?"

Amanda looked at the other woman. Sarah's eyes held none of the usual emotions she'd come to expect when hearing that question - someone asking out of vulgar curiosity, disbelief, or just because they were bored. Instead, she looked as if she cared. Maybe that was what let Amanda answer honestly.

"I was scared," she said. "Scared of hurting a patient by mistake. Scared of loving my patients, because what would I do then if something went wrong?"

Sarah nodded her head in commiseration. "I completely understand."

"Oh?"

"Amanda, motherhood is the most frightening thing. The most wonderful thing, sure, but it's terrifying. I never know if I'm doing anything right. Am I giving the boys what they need to grow up to be men of God, or am

145

I making mistakes that are going to harm them later in life?" She shook her head. "And you just never know. There are no good answers."

"Wow," said Amanda. "I guess I'd really never thought about parenthood that way before."

"And that's even before taking into account Ethan's health problems. You want to talk about scary?" Sarah sighed. "Sometimes I don't think I can handle it."

"But you always seem so calm," said Amanda.

"I don't always feel it."

"I had no idea," said Amanda. She paused and then asked, "How do you handle it?"

Sarah looked at her. "I pray," she said simply. "It's the only thing I know how to do."

Amanda swallowed. "And that helps?"

"It's pretty much the only thing that does. I've found that I can't always control my circumstances – well, I can never control my circumstances," she amended with a laugh, "but if I turn to God, he turns my attitude to what it needs to be." She shrugged. "And I'm able to make it through another day. Fear and all."

Amanda listened thoughtfully. She'd been skeptical at first that Sarah could understand the kind of fear she was talking about, but after listening, she realized she'd been shortsighted. Maybe she was wrong to feel that the fear she felt was something that kept her apart from other people. Maybe everyone had to deal with fear in some way or another.

Sarah's voice broke into her thoughts. "Look who I see. The prodigal son returns."

Amanda peered down the street to see Daniel coming towards them.

Sarah stood. "I think I'll leave you two alone."

"Ok," said Amanda. "Tell Kyle and the boys I said hello. And, Sarah," Sarah turned to her, "thanks for the advice."

Sarah leaned down and gave Amanda a quick hug. "Anytime, sweetie."

Sarah gave Daniel a wave as she headed back to her car.

Daniel came up as Sarah was pulling away.

"What was Sarah doing here?" he asked, dropping onto the swing next to Amanda.

"Giving me therapy," joked Amanda, reaching out for his hand. He grasped her fingers tightly. "Where have you been?" she asked.

He raised his eyebrows. "Believe it or not, I actually went to a Bible study group this evening."

She looked surprised, but pleased. "Really? I thought you couldn't make time for that."

"Let's just say that an old friend showed me the error of my ways." He smiled. "Ernie gave me a very serious talk about a willful horse." He snorted. "I'm pretty sure I was the horse."

Amanda laughed out loud at that. "Well how was the study group?" she asked when she stopped laughing.

"Good," said Daniel thoughtfully. "We were reading from Psalms tonight. One verse really struck me." He looked at her and quoted, "'It is better to take refuge in the Lord than to trust in man.'"

She looked at him questioningly.

"I have a feeling," he continued, "that I've only trusted in man. This man, right here," he said, pointing at himself, "to be specific."

Amanda leaned her head on his shoulder and let him continue to share.

"I've been relying on myself, on my hard work, on my abilities, rather than on God. Not that I don't have to do any work, but I've got to remember that I'm not doing anything out of my own strength. I'm doing it through his. And he will help me." He wrapped his arm around her. "After all, he sent me you, didn't he?"

Amanda smiled. She'd never heard Daniel speak so openly about his faith, and the words drew her to him more than anything else she'd encountered about him.

"Sounds like you got a lot out of the meeting," she said. "I'm glad you went."

"I am, too. I should have gone months ago." He looked down at her. "How are you doing?"

Amanda admired the diplomatic way he spoke. He could have just as easily asked how she was feeling since she freaked out and ran away so she wouldn't have to talk to him. It was probably a closer description of what had actually happened.

"Good," she said and took a deep breath. "Listen, I'm sorry I left so suddenly after work today. As you may have noticed, I sometimes run away when I don't want to discuss something."

"Never noticed," he said lightly. When she gave him a skeptical look, he amended, "Ok, maybe I have. Once or twice."

"But you deserve better than that," she said, "I'm sorry."

Daniel kissed the top of her head where it lay on his shoulder. "Apology accepted."

Amanda steeled herself to continue. "I was a little thrown by our conversation this morning, and, the truth is, I don't know what the future holds. I'm not even sure what I want." She sat up to look at him. "Well, that's not entirely true. I know that I want to enjoy every second of this week with you. Beth is reviewing the report now, and we should hear her verdict in a couple days. In the meantime, let's try to forget about the future and just have fun together." She swallowed nervously. "What do you say?"

He leaned down and gently kissed her lips, as soft as a whisper. "I say yes."

DANIEL WAS as good as his word. He and Amanda spent the next several days in a sort of honeymoon. They spent the weekend in each other's constant company and then kept it up during the workweek. They worked with each other during the day, collaborating on patients and laughing in his office. They spent the evenings taking picnics and going for long walks down the streets of Highland Canyon. They spent one night back at Kyle and Sarah's home, enjoying the company of his family and the sweet snuggles from Robert and Ethan.

They rarely spoke about the grant. He wondered occasionally when they would hear from Beth, to get her final seal of approval, but he didn't bring it up. He didn't want to spook Amanda again, choosing to instead enjoy the time they had together.

And Amanda seemed to be enjoying it too. She was in an awesome mood every morning and ready to hit the ground running with patients.

She shocked him one morning when she announced that she'd asked Ben Fitzgerald to come back in to the office.

"But," said Daniel, nonplussed, "I thought you didn't want to treat him. You said allergies were a trigger for you."

Amanda shook her head. "I was being silly. I looked over his records earlier. I really think I can help him. If it's ok with you."

"Please," said Daniel. "Be my guest." And he watched with amazement as she strode into Ben's room.

Yes, every day was a treasure, made all the sweeter because he didn't know how many more he would have with her.

When she walked into his office Thursday morning with her eyes shining brightly, he knew something had happened.

He stood up quickly, arrested by her expression.

"Did you hear from Beth?" he asked urgently.

She nodded. "I had an email waiting for me this morning."

"And?"

"She approves of the grant!" yelped Amanda. "She's going to take it to the Board!"

Daniel's mouth dropped open. "So quickly? Just like that, it's approved?"

"Technically, she's still got to get the rest of the Board to agree, but trust me, if Beth endorses it, you've got the grant. The Board does everything she says."

Daniel gave a whoop and crossed to Amanda. She threw her arms around Daniel as he lifted her up into the air. He spun her around twice before he kissed her fiercely. His hands tangled in her hair as he put into the kiss all the grateful feelings that he couldn't find the words for.

When they finally pulled apart, Amanda's face was shining with happiness. "We did it," she said. "You're going to get your clinic. Ethan's going to have the care he needs."

"Thanks to you," said Daniel, looking down into her shining eyes.

His new clinic. It was finally going to happen. His head swam with the possibilities that were now before him, but they all converged on one point – Ethan. He knew the center would help countless people, but right then, it was his sweet nephew who was in his thoughts. Finally, Ethan could receive the care he needed. His future suddenly looked much brighter.

"Thank you, Jesus," Daniel murmured.

He clasped Amanda tightly to his heart, thinking of how much we owed to this woman. How on earth was he ever supposed to let her go?

CHAPTER 10

Amanda fixed her hair excitedly that evening. Daniel was taking her out for dinner to celebrate, though he wouldn't give her the details. He would only say that it was going to be fun.

"Wear that pretty dress you wore on the first night we went to Kyle's house. The white one," he'd said

Amanda raised her eyebrows. "I can't believe you remember what I wore on a specific night."

He growled and nuzzled her hair. "Like I could forget how you looked in that dress."

She'd laughed and swatted him away, but, tonight, she'd pulled out the dress immediately.

When she was ready, she ran downstairs to wait for him.

The street was surprisingly busy that night, with lots of cars pulling up in front of the diner. Amanda watched curiously as several couples exited their vehicles and walked inside the restaurant. She could hear strains of music drifting out every time the door was opened. What was going on?

Finally, Daniel arrived, looking handsome in dark jeans and a plaid shirt. His eyes sought her out, and she watched his gaze intensify to the point that all the gold seemed to disappear.

"You look beautiful," he said, taking both of her hands. "Not that I'm surprised."

"Thank you," she said. "You look pretty amazing yourself."

"I had to up my game. After all, I was going out with the best looking woman in town tonight."

"And where are we going?"

Daniel smiled. "We're going to take a long walk. About, oh, ten feet."

Amanda laughed. "So we're going to the diner. I might have known."

He slipped his arm around her waist and led her next door. "But this is not the diner you know and love. Wait until you see."

When they walked inside the diner, Amanda understood what he was talking about. First of all, the place was packed. Couples filled almost every available seat. Music was playing and the lights were lower than usual. Several tables had been cleared away, making an already crowded seating situation worse.

"We'll never get a table," said Amanda. "What are all these people doing here?"

"Don't worry," said Daniel. "I've got a connection." He waved across the room to Millie, where she was bantering with some customers. As soon as she saw Daniel and Amanda, she ran over to greet them.

"Welcome to Diner Date Night," she said, giving Amanda a quick hug. "Sweetie, you look fantastic!" She turned to Daniel. "Dr. Shane, I've got your table like you requested."

Amanda looked at her with a raised eyebrow. "You do reservations in your diner?"

"Only when I really like the customer," she said. "Now come on." She led them through a crowded room to a corner booth. Amanda recognized it as the same booth where she'd sat with Millie after she and Daniel almost kissed on art day. She gave Millie a sly smile as she slid into her seat.

Millie winked back and whispered, "I knew you'd like sitting here. It was too perfect to pass up." She then hurried off to tend to other customers, leaving behind a suspicious Daniel.

"What was that about?" he asked, joining her across the table.

"Oh, nothing," said Amanda lightly. She looked around. "Diner Date Night? That's a pretty fun idea."

"People are always talking it up as a good time," said Daniel. "I thought we could give it a try."

"Haven't you ever been before?"

"Nope." He smiled at her. "I haven't dated much in recent years."

Amanda glanced around the room. "That explains the stares we're getting."

"They're looking at you."

Amanda laughed. "Who knew you were such a sweet talker?" She reached over to the head of the table to grab a menu. "So, what are you going to get?"

Daniel picked the menu out of her hands. "No ordering tonight. We all get the same thing."

"Oh," said Amanda, vaguely disappointed. "What do we get?"

Daniel grinned. "Everything."

And he was right. Within minutes, waiters whisked around the room depositing plates and silverware on the various tables. Then they began the rounds with huge pots of family style dishes. They went from table to table, giving out helpings of all of the diner's most popular meals.

Amanda was in heaven as she sampled bison burgers, sweet corn on the cob, pot roast, green beans, elk sliders, and a huckleberry tart.

As she finished off the tart, Daniel looked at her in amazement. "Where are you putting all that food?"

"Are there any more huckleberries?" she asked, looking around for a waiter. "That was scrumptious."

Suddenly, the lights went dimmed further.

"Sorry," said Daniel, "we'll have to hunt down more dessert in a little while. The next portion of the evening is beginning." He slid out of the booth and stood by her, holding out his hand expectantly. She grabbed it and climbed out to follow him.

Amanda looked around the room, noticing that other couples were doing the same. She spotted Sarah and Kyle across the room.

"Look, Sarah and Kyle are here," she said, waving at them. Sarah smiled and waved back, and Amanda noticed Kyle wiggling his eyebrows at Daniel.

"What a goofball," said Daniel, though he was smiling. "Come on, let's swing by and tell them the good news."

They crossed the crowd to join the other couple.

Sarah gave Amanda a hug. "You look lovely, Amanda."

"So do you," said Amanda, noting the other woman's shining complexion. "You're downright glowing!"

Sarah laughed. "That's what a night out will for you when you have twins at home."

Daniel broke in. "Are you ready to feel even happier?" He laid an arm across Amanda's shoulders. "Thanks to my beautiful date's amazing grant report, we just received word that the grant is a go." Sarah gasped, and Daniel continued. "We're going to be able to build the new clinic."

Kyle grabbed Daniel's hand and pounded him on the back, while Sarah gripped Amanda's arms as if she needed to steady herself.

"I can't believe it," said Kyle. "You really did it, man."

"Praise God," said Sarah, shaking her head. "What a blessing that's going to be. For all of us."

"And especially for Ethan," said Daniel. "You don't have to worry about getting him the care that he needs ever again."

Sarah's eyes filled with tears, and Amanda noticed that even Kyle looked misty. He wrapped an arm around his wife, and she leaned her head on his shoulder. Wordlessly, peace seemed to radiate off of them.

Amanda had watched the interaction between the three of them with a warm glow of accomplishment. This was the first time that she'd ever become so involved in a grant, and the feeling of satisfaction was made all the greater by knowing how they would all be impacted for the good.

"Ok, enough of this talking," said Daniel, turning to Amanda. "Come on. Let's leave these two to blubber together. We're getting in the way." He grabbed her hand, and together they threaded through the crowd to the cleared area of the room.

Slowly, the music volume rose, a sweet, slow song filling the air.

"Care to dance?" Daniel asked with a crooked grin.

Amanda happily stepped into his arms.

Together they swayed to the music. Amanda lost track of who all was on the dance floor with them. She only had eyes for the kind, generous man holding her in his arms.

They danced through song after song, and slowly the playful and celebratory mood of the evening deepened into something more significant.

When Daniel finally spoke again, Amanda was surprised to hear that his voice was husky and low. She could feel his words with every part of her body as well as hear them.

"Amanda," he said, "I want you to know what a blessing it's been to have you here."

She closed her eyes and leaned her head against him, taking in the indefinable scent that was Daniel. Dancing there with him, it was hard to remember that she ever had to leave. Surely, they could stay like that forever, endlessly turning in each other's arms.

She sighed. She was so happy, a feeling unmixed for once with any anxiety or fear. She felt a joy welling up inside of her that she knew all came from this man.

Amanda turned her face up to smile at him. "Thank you for tonight," she said. "It's the best celebration I could have thought of."

Daniel's gaze intensified, and Amanda found herself watching him in fascination. She almost wanted to reach up and touch his face to make sure that he was real.

"Amanda," he said, "I don't know what the future holds for us. But I'd be kicking myself if I let you leave without telling you this."

"Telling me what?" asked Amanda, dimly noticing that somewhere along the line they'd stopped moving.

He put his hand to her face and ran his thumb along her jawline. He looked as though he were drinking in the sight of her.

"Tell you that I love you."

Amanda's eyes widened. She'd forgotten about the other dancers, almost forgotten about the world itself. "You love me?" she asked.

Daniel nodded. "Desperately."

Amanda obeyed her heart and reached up to kiss him. He responded in kind, kissing her with a gentle passion that left her head spinning. When they finally released one another, it was only to the dim awareness of some sort of noise.

Amanda looked around, dazed, and noticed several people looking at them. No, scratch that, everyone was looking and... applauding?

The entire room was cheering them on. Amanda's felt heat rush to her face as she saw the delighted faces of all the other customers. She spotted Millie jumping up and down in a corner. Sarah was clasping her hands and smiling, and Kyle was downright whooping.

Amanda buried her face in Daniel's shoulder.

"I am going to die," she said.

He wrapped an arm around her. "Sorry about this," he murmured. "But on the bright side, I guess I definitely proved to you that I don't date much. We brought down the house."

Amanda took a deep breath and lifted her head. She couldn't help laughing at the expressions on everyone's faces. She gave a little wave, and the crowd just clapped the harder.

"All right, nothing to see here," said Daniel.

"I don't know about that, Dr. Shane," someone yelled from the crowd, which started up the laughing again.

Amanda scanned the crowd, looking for the best escape route. She'd put a brave face on, but now she was ready to hide her head.

And maybe continue that kiss.

She was about to suggest to Daniel that it was time that they leave when she froze. She tightened her grip on Daniel's arm. She felt the room start to spin again.

But this time, it wasn't a kiss that did it.

She was looking at a newcomer who stood by the door, staring at her with the same kind of shock Amanda was feeling.

It was Beth Weisman, her boss, come to Highland Canyon.

DANIEL WAS only marginally surprised when Amanda took off for the door. For all her talk about stopping her habit of escaping, that had been pretty embarrassing. He didn't mind one bit her wanting to leave.

But he did want to know why she didn't bring him with her.

"Amanda!" he called, chasing her out into the street. "Where are you –" He stopped abruptly when he was confronted by a scene he hadn't expected.

Amanda stood in the street facing another woman. She was older, dressed in a frumpy black suit and dragging a rolling suitcase. He could feel the tension between the two women rolling over him in waves.

Whoever this was, Amanda did not look happy to see her.

The stranger turned to him with a stern expression. "Dr. Daniel Shane, I presume?"

He nodded in confusion. "That's me. And you are?"

"Beth Weisman," she said in clipped tones. "Perhaps you've heard of me?"

"Of course," said Daniel, walking forward to greet her. She stared at his outstretched hand, unmoving, until he finally dropped it. "It's very nice to meet you in person," he continued uncertainly. "Amanda has told me so much about you and your family. The work you do at the Weisman Trust is truly an inspiration."

Beth stared at him for a moment with a hard expression. Finally, she turned back to Amanda and addressed her as if Daniel had never spoken.

"Is there somewhere we can speak privately, Amanda?"

Despite the panic that Daniel could see in her eyes, Amanda spoke calmly. "You can speak freely in front of Dr. Shane, Beth."

"Yes, I can see that," said Beth after a moment. "You two have obviously gotten close during your time in this town."

"What are you doing here?" Amanda asked.

Beth drew herself up. "Your report was so glowing, I wanted to see this man's practice for myself. The way you described it, it sounded truly remarkable." She glanced at the diner. "Of course, after that display, I think I know why."

"And why is that?" asked Amanda in a steely voice.

"Your feelings have obviously colored your judgment."

Daniel couldn't believe his ears. Was she accusing Amanda of favoritism?

"So sorry I couldn't have given you warning," Beth said in a sarcastic voice, "but I couldn't get my cell phone to work on the way here. Then you could have been ready to hide your romance."

"I wouldn't have hidden anything," said Amanda, "because we haven't done anything to be ashamed of."

"You know my rule, Amanda."

Daniel saw Amanda raise her chin. "Yes, I do. And I freely admit that I broke it by dating Daniel. But there was no other impropriety. I've lived in this town for a month now, and there isn't a person in it who wouldn't stand up for him or tell you about the good he's done."

She continued, fire lighting in her eyes. "I've seen the need in the community for a new clinic with my own eyes. I've even treated some of those patients myself." She raised her hands in supplication. "Isn't that why you asked me to stay on for longer? So that I could really understand the situation?"

"I asked you to stay on for longer because I thought it would help you make a better decision. Clearly, that was a mistake. It clouded your judgment and allowed you to become too involved in their lives."

"How can we be too involved, Beth? We're not robots."

Daniel watched their exchange in tense silence. He wanted to stand up for Amanda and argue her case, but, listening to her talk, he realized that he didn't need to. Amanda had this.

Beth drew herself up. "I don't think that asking you to maintain some objectivity is expecting you to be a robot, Amanda."

Amanda paused. "You're right. I'm sorry. But I want you to see that because I became involved in the life of Highland Canyon, that is what has allowed me to really understand this project."

"That was the idea," said Beth, "but you took it too far." She threw her hands in the air and seemingly spoke to herself. "See if I ever try this experiment again! From now on, we go in, assess, and get out within the week. I can't have my staff kissing every grantee in the West."

"That's a bit of an exaggeration," muttered Amanda.

Beth looked up at the pair of them.

Amanda spoke again, firmly. "I didn't fabricate that report, Beth. Everything I told you is absolutely true."

Beth's expression seemed to soften slightly. "Maybe it is, Amanda. I hope so, at any rate. But I can't possibly recommend this grant to the Board now. You must see that. Your entire credibility is in doubt."

She turned to look at Daniel, finally acknowledging his presence again. He thought he detected a note of pity, but it wasn't enough to soften the blow of her words.

"I regret to inform you, Dr. Shane, that your grant has been denied by the Weisman Trust." She turned to Amanda, and, this time, the pity was very evident. "And, I'm sorry, Amanda," she continued. "You're fired."

AMANDA WATCHED in shock as Beth walked towards the Ten Trees Inn, her suitcase bumping along behind her.

"I guess she's staying the night," she said, hardly knowing what she was saying. "It beats spending the night on the road, I suppose, with the wolves. And bears. And coyotes." She looked at Daniel. "Did I ever tell you that I heard a wolf on the night I first got here? It was very scary."

"Amanda?" Daniel asked tentatively. "Are you ok?"

"Nobody's ok with wolves around." She couldn't stop talking. If she did, she'd be forced to acknowledge the terrible thing that had happened. If she just kept talking, then it wouldn't be true. "What do you think? Should we head back in to date night? Sounds like the music is still going. Let's dance some more. That would be fun."

Daniel walked to her and carefully grabbed her arm. "You're in shock, Amanda."

"No, I'm not. I want to dance. And eat. You promised we'd find another huckleberry tart. We still need to do that."

"Let's sit down," said Daniel.

Why was he looking at her like that? Like she was about to break. She was fine. Just fine.

He walked her across the street to his building. He settled her on the porch swing and sat beside her.

He didn't speak though, and Amanda found that she suddenly lost all of her words as well. So they sat together in silence.

Amanda couldn't say how long they stayed that way, listening to the faint strains of music and laughter coming from Millie's.

Amanda couldn't believe how much had changed in so short a time. Was it only that evening that Daniel told her that he loved her?

She glanced at him. He didn't look like a man in love now. And who could blame him? She'd just lost him his medical center.

Why did she ever become involved with him? He didn't know Beth, didn't know how strict she was. But she did. She should have seen this coming.

But instead, she was happy to go along with her feelings for Daniel. Happy to fall in love with him.

For she knew now that she did love him. She'd resisted the admission for weeks, but she knew. She loved him.

How tragic that she only realized it now, when it appeared to be too late.

And what about her? She thought ironically that she used to have too many options for her future. Now, she had none. She'd lost Daniel; she'd lost her job. What should she do now?

And still, Daniel didn't speak.

DANIEL'S THOUGHTS were reeling.

The grant was gone, and with it, all his plans for the medical center. Everything he'd worked for for the past two years.

He supposed he could try again with a different foundation. The Weisman Trust wasn't the only organization that supported healthcare initiatives. But it would mean starting all over again.

And even if he did find another willing funder, the project would be necessarily delayed. How much longer would his patients go without the proper care that they needed? How long did they have until Ethan needed more serious medical intervention? What would they do if something happened in the meantime?

He looked at Amanda. She looked terrible. Daniel guiltily realized that he'd been so focused on the loss of the grant that he'd ignored what had happened to her.

Amanda had lost her job. He knew how much it meant to her, and now it was gone. Because of him.

No wonder she looked so unhappy here with him.

I did that, he thought. If only he'd listened to her the first time she said no to dating. She'd still have the career that she wanted. What good was loving her if it cost her the life that she wanted? He felt selfish for ever interfering.

Daniel wanted to reach his arm around her and hold her. But he was afraid that she'd push him away.

And he'd deserve it if she did.

After a moment, Amanda slowly pushed off of the swing and stood. She turned to Daniel. All the shock seemed to have worn off; now she just looked tired.

"I'm going to go back to the hotel," she said.

He nodded. "I understand. Can I walk you back?"

She shook her head. "I think I'd rather be alone right now. I need time to think." She started down the stairs, but paused when she reached the bottom. She half-turned back in his direction. "Thank you for the lovely evening. Until… you know."

And with that, she turned back around and walked straight to the hotel.

Daniel watched her go with a sinking heart. He didn't know how they could ever come back from this. Would she ever forgive him for costing her her job?

He stayed on the swing a few more minutes, wracked with equal parts self-blame and self-pity. He couldn't believe he'd lost the clinic. He couldn't believe he'd lost Amanda.

He heard a burst of laughter from the diner across the street. He thought of Sarah and Kyle, happily dancing together inside with no idea of the damage that had been done.

Daniel buried his face in his hands. If only he'd never told them that the grant was on. They'd have been disappointed to find out the grant wasn't approved, but they would have understood. But this, this was worse. This false victory, for them to think that Ethan would have the care he needed, only to have the rug pulled out from under them. It was cruel.

He sat on that swing, surrounded by playground equipment that seemed to be mocking him with its lighthearted feel, and felt sorry for himself. Slowly rocking back and forth, he indulged in every guilty feeling imaginable. Finally, though, he shook himself out of his lethargy and tried to think clearly. There had to be a way to fix his problems. There always was. He'd started his pediatric office in the Montana wilderness and made it flourish through the work of his own two hands. He'd researched and sought out the Weisman Trust as a potential way to fund the new clinic. No one else had done that for him.

He needed now to apply that same can-do attitude. There was nothing he couldn't accomplish if he worked hard enough.

He jumped off the swing and unlocked the front door of his practice. Striding through the dark waiting room, he went back to his private office, switched on the light, and turned on the computer. As he waited for the system to boot up, he started running through options in his mind.

He'd start by researching other organizations that made healthcare grants. There was every possibility that he could find one that would be interested in funding his new clinic. Maybe they'd even have a job opening that Amanda could try for. She wouldn't be here with him, unfortunately, but it would give her what she wanted – her career.

His mind was whirling with ideas and strategies. He felt energized, back in comfortable territory. He had a big problem ahead of him, but he thrived in challenging situations. He'd just work his way through to the other side. He could do this, he repeated to himself over and over again.

Suddenly, sitting in the glow of his computer's screen, about to start typing in the internet search bar, he stopped.

I can do this. I can do this. I can do this.

The refrain echoed through his head. Why did it sound… wrong?

He pulled his hands away from his keyboard.

Unbidden, a new phrase popped into his head. "It is better to take refuge in the Lord than to trust in man."

He was doing it again, relying on himself instead of on God's protection.

But it was a huge problem, he told himself, with no easy solution. If he didn't take action, how would the clinic be built?

It was almost as if he felt another part of him answer. *By trusting in the Lord.*

He sat in silence for several minutes, the two sides of himself warring with each other. Finally, Daniel slowly reached up and turned the computer monitor off. He pushed back from his desk, rose, and quietly left the building. As he locked the front door behind him, he looked up to the sky.

I'm trusting in you, Lord. This one is in your hands.

AMANDA NUMBLY entered the lobby of the Inn. Even inside the hotel, she could hear the music faintly from next door. She was glad someone was still having fun.

She walked up to the front desk to speak to the attendant on duty, the same young lady who'd been working the first night Amanda came to Highland Canyon.

"Good evening," Amanda said, trying to smile. "I believe an older woman came through here a little while ago. Did she check in?"

"She did," said the clerk. "Did you need her?"

"I'll try her on the phone," said Amanda. She strove to sound casual. "What's her room number?"

The attendant glanced at her records book. "Room 31."

"Thanks," said Amanda, mentally filing the information. "Have a good night."

"You too."

As Amanda trudged down the hall to her room, she passed number 31. She could hear the TV blaring inside. Amanda knew that Beth liked to lose herself in movies when she was upset. And it sounded like she was definitely upset.

Amanda passed on, unable to face her boss. *Well, ex-boss*, she thought. She wanted to talk to her and plead her case, but she knew instinctively that it wouldn't do any good. Not unless she had some reason to make Beth believe that Amanda's report hadn't been colored by her feelings for Daniel.

Amanda slipped inside her room. She found herself staring dully at Rita's picture of Daniel and Amanda with all the cats. With a sob that she struggled to keep in, she pulled it from the wall and placed it facedown on the dresser. She couldn't look at it right then.

She took a deep breath. She had to keep it together. Falling apart wouldn't help anything.

Her thoughts on Beth kept running through her brain. If only there were some way to convince her boss of how great the new clinic really would be. And how needed it was in the community.

But what could she do?

Remembering how angry Beth was, Amanda threw out any idea that involved Beth seeing the clinic for herself. She knew for sure that Beth would be out of town first thing in the morning.

That gave Amanda one night to prove the clinic's worth. She gave a hollow laugh. Not doable.

She lay back on the bed and stared blankly up, trying to twist her brain into giving her some sort of idea.

Maybe she could rally the town to come to her aid. She knew how highly Daniel was thought of. Maybe people would be willing to come out in the morning and take a stand for the clinic before Beth left.

Amanda had a mental image of Beth walking out to her car and meeting a crowd of strangers, all of whom wanted her to give the clinic another chance. She might be moved by the town's support... Or she might just be angry at being put on the spot in that way. Amanda sighed. Better not try it and make things worse.

Could Amanda go over Beth's head and speak to the Board of Directors directly? She briefly considered the possibility before rejecting it. Beth might not be on the Board of the Weisman Trust, but she still was the one with all the influence. The higher-ups would do whatever she said.

For one second, Amanda entertained the idea of offering to give up her job in exchange for the grant moving forward again. But then she remembered the ugly truth –that she'd been fired and had no job to bargain with.

She had never felt so powerless.

Well, Lord, she thought, *I'm at a loss. I'm too scared to be a doctor, and apparently I'm also a failure as a grants officer. What do you want me to fail at next?*

Maybe she'd try teaching next. If she didn't want to be a doctor herself, she could still train others in medicine. Dr. Kowalski certainly seemed to find it a rewarding career.

She must really be enjoying her new role, thought Amanda. Placing students in their internships would appeal to her. She was all about having her students try new things and learn from them.

Thinking of Dr. Kowalski reminded her of a particularly memorable speech that her professor once made. Amanda could picture her now, standing at the front of the room on Amanda's first day of medical school.

"Some of you look a little frightened," Dr. Kowalski had said, as nervous laughter rippled through the room. "Perhaps you are thinking, what have I gotten myself into?"

More laughter.

Dr. Kowalski smiled. "And you're right to think that. Because you are in for a wild ride. But I tell you now, fear is good. It's our extremely rational response to what can be scary situations. You'll encounter some of those in your practices – I know I have. But when the fear comes, you'll know that I will have prepared you in every way I can to beat that fear and do the impossible in spite of it." She spread her arms wide. "And that is exactly what you will do."

Lying on her hotel bed, Amanda wondered if that is what she would be able to do. Could she pull off the impossible?

Slowly, she started to get the germ of an idea. She sat up straighter, running through the possibilities in her head. It was a long shot. It might not ever make it past the idea stage. But if it worked, she might just have a chance of saving the clinic.

She grabbed her phone. It was time to call Dr. Kowalski.

CHAPTER 11

Amanda took a deep breath and steeled herself for an uncomfortable conversation. It was the next morning. She'd risen well before her normal time to make sure she didn't miss Beth's departure. Weak early morning light was streaming through the window at the end of the hall. Amanda offered up a quick prayer for fortitude before doing what she had to do.

Quietly, she knocked on Beth's door.

The door swung open after a minute.

"Oh, it's you," said Beth. "I wondered who'd be here at this hour." In spite of the time, she was already dressed for the day.

"Can I come in?" asked Amanda.

Beth sighed and opened the door wider. "Come on."

Amanda followed her inside the room gratefully. Inside, Beth motioned her to the room's desk chair, while she sat on the edge of the bed.

Amanda took the seat indicated. She glanced around the room. Beth's suitcase was lying already packed on the bed. So she'd been right to be here so early. Beth was planning a quick getaway.

Amanda noticed that Beth's anger from the night before seemed to have cooled somewhat. The older woman sat looking at her now with a hint of compassion in her eyes, though Amanda still could see the steely resolve that she'd expected.

"You know I can't change my mind about the grant," said Beth.

"I understand where you're coming from."

Beth shook her head. "Amanda, what were you thinking?" She threw her hands in the air. "You know the rule. Never get involved with a grantee. *Never*. It doesn't end well."

Amanda swallowed. "I'm very sorry that I disappointed you, Beth. That wasn't my intention."

Beth looked at her sadly. "I know it wasn't. But it was still a serious lapse in judgment." She sighed. "Did you come here to ask for your job back?"

"No," said Amanda. "I'm here in my capacity as the grants officer who has worked this project for the last month." She held up her hand to stop Beth from interrupting, as she seemed likely to do. "Don't worry. I understand that I am an *unemployed* grants officer. But I still know more about this proposed medical center than anyone. And I know that it's a perfect fit for the Weisman Trust."

Beth sighed. "It seemed that way from your report. But you have to see, I can't trust anything in there now." She frowned. "I know you didn't fabricate anything, Amanda, but how much of your view was clouded by your infatuation with Dr. Shane?"

"It's not an infatuation," said Amanda calmly.

Beth looked skeptical. "However you would characterize it, your credibility is compromised."

Amanda took a deep breath. "I understand. What if I could pull in an outside source to vouch for Dr. Shane and for the new project? Someone whom you couldn't suspect of an ulterior motive."

Beth crossed her arms. "I suppose I'd be willing to listen. But it would have to be a pretty strong endorsement to overcome my reservations."

Amanda steadied her nerves. This was the make-or-break moment.

"You've heard of Dr. Kowalski at Washington State, I presume."

"Yes, of course I have. She's one of the best-known doctors in our state." Beth raised one eyebrow. "Are you saying that Dr. Kowalski wants to vouch for him?" When Amanda nodded, Beth continued, "I'm still not sure that's enough. A recommendation is easy enough to give."

"It's more than just a recommendation," Amanda went on. "Dr. Kowalski is currently in charge of placing medical students in their third-year internships. She has agreed to include the new Highland Canyon clinic as a site for her students. Once the center is up and running, she will place 3-5 medical students here at a time to work in the clinic."

"Hmm." Beth seemed intrigued, and Amanda felt her hopes rise. "What's her reasoning behind this?"

"First," said Amanda, "because she believes, as do I, that there is a serious lack of training for doctors in rural sites. It would be a valuable opportunity for her students to learn about practicing outside of cities, and she wants to broaden their horizons.

"Second," she went on, and here her voice softened, "because she believes in Dr. Shane and the work he is doing. She's mentored him for the last few years, and she knows what an asset he is in this region. She's ready to talk to you about him. I've notified her that you might be calling her to get her opinion on the new clinic."

Beth gave her an appraising look. "You arranged all this on your own, since last night?"

Amanda nodded.

"That's going above and beyond. Especially since, as you say, you are an *unemployed* grant officer."

"I know I shook your faith in me, Beth. And I'm sorry about that. But I had to undo the damage I caused. The people of this area shouldn't have to go without the medical care they need, solely because of my actions."

Beth sat silently for a moment, and Amanda sat in tense expectation of her answer. When she finally did speak, Amanda let out a breath she hadn't realized she'd been holding.

"Ok," said Beth. "Assuming Dr. Kowalski confirms your report, the grant is back on the table. I will bring it along with your recommendation to the Board."

Amanda felt a surge of joy. She jumped out of her chair and hugged Beth. "Oh, thank you! You won't be sorry, I promise. It's a great opportunity for the town and for the Trust."

Beth patted her back. "Ok, ok. Get off me. I have something else to say." Amanda immediately pulled away and went back to her chair. She was almost bouncing with excitement.

Beth eyed her. "I'm impressed at what you pulled off here. That was some quick thinking, and, in spite of what I think about your personal decisions while here, I do think you have the best interests of the Trust in mind.

"I'm still disappointed in your behavior, mind you." She added almost to herself, "And see if I ever try this experiment again! No more staying too long to work in any one spot." She looked at Amanda. "But I take back my words from last night. Let's just forget that you were ever fired."

Amanda sat in shock. "Really?"

Beth nodded, but then fixed her with a stern eye. "However, I do expect you back at the office immediately. You can say your goodbyes this morning, but then I want you back on the road. There's a 2:30 flight from Great

Falls to Seattle this afternoon, and I expect you to be on it."

"I will." Amanda stood up. "Thank you, Beth. I appreciate the second chance."

Beth harrumphed. "You're a good worker, Amanda. I hated to have to let you go."

Amanda stayed with her boss as she checked out and then accompanied her outside

As they exited the hotel, Ernie passed by on his way into the diner. He tipped his cowboy hat at Beth and winked at Amanda as he walked silently by.

"Goodness," said Beth, momentarily stopping on the sidewalk. "There are some good-looking men in this town."

Amanda stifled a laugh as she walked Beth to her car.

"Remember," said Beth, sounding as businesslike as ever. "2:30."

Amanda watched as Beth drove off. She couldn't believe that she'd pulled it off. Daniel would get the grant, and she could go back to her career.

So why didn't she feel happier?

She glanced across the street. She imagined that Daniel would probably already be at work for the day. She sighed. Time for the hardest conversation of the day.

"KNOCK, KNOCK."

Daniel looked up from his work. "Amanda," he said, feeling a rush of relief. "I wasn't sure if you were going to come in today."

"Me either," admitted Amanda. "I wasn't sure if you'd want me to."

"I always want you here," said Daniel seriously. He walked towards her and took her hands. "Listen, I know last night was a setback. But we can find a way through. I'm sure of it." He struggled with finding the right words to explain the certainty that he felt inside. "I think God's got it," he said, finally.

Amanda raised her eyebrows. "I didn't expect those words to ever come from you."

Daniel smiled. "Fair enough. But I really do feel at peace. Like it's going to work out somehow. I just don't know how."

Amanda nodded. "I know how."

He gave her a quizzical look. "What do you mean?"

He listened in increasingly stunned silence as she described the plan with Dr. Kowalski, and the deal she'd struck with Beth.

"So," she finished up, "assuming everything I've arranged is ok with you, the grant should be back on the fast track."

Daniel could only stare at her.

Amanda suddenly looked concerned. "I hope I didn't overstep my bounds. It's just that we'd already discussed how you'd be short-staffed until the clinic started to attract new personnel. So I thought we could accelerate that part of the process, get some help early, and convince Beth in the process." She gave him a tentative glance. "What do you think?"

Daniel reached out and pulled her into his arms. He buried his face in her hair, holding her tightly against his pounding heart.

"You did it," he whispered.

"So I take it you approve?" She sounded amused.

"How could I not? It's a brilliant solution. I can't believe you went to all that trouble for me."

Amanda pulled back and laughed. "It's not like it was a hard sell. Dr. Kowalski loves you."

"Make light of it all you want," he said. "I know that couldn't have been an easy conversation to have with Beth. Especially after she fired you."

Amanda sighed. "Yeah, it was uncomfortable."

Daniel noticed an odd expression cross Amanda's face as she said it. "Did anything else happen?" he asked carefully.

"Yes." Amanda gave a faint smile. "Beth gave me my job back."

Daniel felt as if a ton of bricks had landed in his lap. "Oh." He took a deep breath and tried to remind himself what this meant to her. "That's great. Really great. She was crazy to let you go in the first place, so I'm glad she saw sense."

"Thanks," Amanda said. "That means a lot to me." She took a deep breath. "She wants me to meet her at the airport this afternoon. Well, it was pretty much an order for me to join her on her flight." She checked her watch. "It's going to take me a couple of hours to get there, so I'm afraid I can't help with patients today."

"Oh. You're leaving today," said Daniel, still trying to process the news.

"I have to," said Amanda apologetically. She touched his hand. "Listen, I know this leaves us in kind of a weird spot. Relationship-wise."

Daniel nodded. Was she about to break his heart?

Amanda continued. "I don't want to give up on us, though. I'm willing to give long distance a chance if you are."

Daniel hesitated. In his admittedly small experience, long distance romances only seemed to work if they were temporary. What was the end game for them? Would they ever live in the same place, or was he fated to stay in Montana and she in Seattle? Long distance romance might work for a while, but you couldn't build a marriage on it.

And looking at Amanda now, he realized that was exactly what he wanted. Marriage to this beautiful, smart, hardworking woman. Who was now going to leave him.

She seemed to have noticed his hesitation. "You don't have to decide right now," she said, looking a little hurt.

"Amanda, I –"

"No, that's ok," she said, holding up her hand to stop him. "I shouldn't have put you on the spot." She backed toward the door. "I need to go pack up my things anyway, or I'll never make it out on time." She paused and gave him a searching look. "I'll come back before I leave town, ok?"

"Ok," said Daniel helplessly. Truthfully, he didn't know what else to say.

She surprised him by coming forward and giving him a light kiss on the cheek. Then she left.

Daniel sank into his chair. The extremes of his emotions from that morning exhausted him. First, the jubilation that the grant was still moving forward, followed so quickly by the sucker punch that Amanda was leaving.

Is this what happens when I trust you? he thought to God.

In spite of his ungrateful words, Daniel felt a peace steal over him. Gradually, he started to see the good sides of the situation.

Last night, Daniel had had the glimmer of hope that Amanda wouldn't leave, but in the cold light of day, he realized that that wasn't the right attitude. He would love for her to choose to stay here with him. But he didn't want her to stay because she was stuck and didn't have anywhere else to go. That wasn't fair to her at all. She'd worked hard for her career and deserved the opportunities that had come her way.

And she was obviously good at what she did. He still couldn't quite believe that the grant was back on. After seeing Beth's face last night, he'd thought there was no way to convince her to give them a second chance. But Amanda had accomplished the impossible within 12 hours. There weren't many women like her.

She'd done her part, and now he felt with a certainty that could only have come from God what he was meant to do next. It was time to make the clinic a reality, and it would take all of his efforts for the next several months to do so.

Well, he amended, his efforts along with God's grace. Daniel had no intention of falling back into his old self-sufficient attitude towards work. He had a huge project ahead of him. And he would finish it by relying on God's strength.

And as for Amanda, he could only give his desires to God and see what would happen. He couldn't make decisions for her, however much he loved her.

"Ok, Lord," he said out loud. "You keep the wheel. And I will trust."

IT TOOK very little time for Amanda to pack up her things. She looked around her hotel room, now totally barren of any stamp of her personality. How could an entire month be so easily erased from a place?

She wondered uncomfortably if everything about her time in Highland Canyon would similarly disappear. Would people even remember her in the years to come?

The children certainly wouldn't. She thought of all the kids she'd examined over the past month. Most of them were too young to retain a memory of her for long. It would be as if she were never here.

And Daniel... What was going to happen with him? She'd recognized the look on his face when she suggested a long distance relationship. He wasn't in favor of it. Yet, she knew that he loved her.

For one moment, she found herself unreasonably angry at him. What was he doing then, letting her just leave? Shouldn't he fight for her and try to convince her not to go? Didn't he want her to stay?

Stay and do what? a small voice in her head asked her.

"I don't know!" she cried out loud. That was the problem. She knew there was a place for her in this town. She could start practicing medicine again full time, first in Daniel's office and later in the new clinic. What she didn't know was if she was ready for that kind of leap of faith.

The past few weeks, practicing medicine had been almost like a holiday. She'd gotten used to it again, but that was ok, because she'd known it was only temporary. She had her nice safe job at the Trust waiting for her.

Could she make the leap to go back to caring for patients fulltime? She knew the reality of being a doctor. The fear would come back at times, the doubts that she might inadvertently harm one of her patients, no matter how safe the case seemed to be. And in a small town like this, where she'd know every one of her patients so well, wouldn't the risk be even greater? She'd never be caring for strangers; they would be friends and neighbors. She just didn't know if she could handle the emotional strain.

You can't, came that small voice again. *Not on your own.*

Amanda paused.

She'd urged Daniel to remember to trust God, to lean on His strength. Was it possible that she needed to listen to her own advice?

She didn't think she could bear her fear on her own. In fact, she knew she couldn't. But what if she surrendered it to God?

Slowly, without a thought beyond that very moment, Amanda sank to her knees, closed her eyes, and offered up a simple prayer.

"Lord," she said out loud, "you know my heart and its weaknesses. You know how scared I can be. Please stay with me and help me to conquer my fear. Help me find the right path."

She wasn't entirely sure what the right path would be, but she was sure God would lead her to it.

DANIEL WAS making notes in a patient chart when Amanda came into his office. He looked up, and his attention was seized by the upbeat expression on her face.

She's really glad to be leaving, he thought dully. The thought hurt, but he made an effort to concentrate on her happiness instead.

"All packed up?" he asked, trying to sound cheerful.

"What?" asked Amanda, looking confused. "Oh, yeah, I am done." She joined him at his desk and perched on the surface beside him. She rubbed her left elbow. "I think I sprained something trying to cram it all back into the suitcase," she said, her green eyes twinkling.

"I guess working for the Trust isn't always so safe after all," Daniel said without thinking. A moment later, he could have clapped a hand across his mouth. Sure, he wasn't happy that she was leaving, but that was no reason to be a jerk about it.

Amanda's eyes seemed to communicate that she knew what was going through his head and that no apology was necessary.

"Do you have a minute to talk?" she asked quietly, "or do you need to get to your patients?"

Daniel pushed back from his desk. "Now's an ok time. We've got a little bit of a lull." What he didn't say was how hard he'd worked to create that lull. He'd been extremely efficient with patients all morning, hoping to create a small window of time so that he could properly say goodbye to Amanda whenever she came by.

Only now that he was faced with the prospect of actually saying it, he wished he were back in with his patients. Anything rather than put on a brave face and pretend he didn't mind that the woman he loved was leaving him.

"Good," said Amanda, slipping her hand into his.

He looked away from her and tried hard to concentrate on anything else. Right then, he didn't want to think about how well her hand fitted into his, or how beautiful she looked with that serene expression.

Darn it, how could she be so peaceful? Didn't she care at all?

Amanda continued, seemingly oblivious to his reluctance to talk. "It's been kind of a weird morning. I can't believe my conversation with Beth was just a couple of hours ago. I feel like I've been through the wringer since then."

"Ha," said Daniel, running his hand over his head, "I know what you mean."

She reached out to smooth his hair back into place. "I'm sorry," she said. "I know I'm part of the reason for that." She took a deep breath. "I was a tad hasty this morning."

Daniel stilled, curious as to what she meant. "In what way?"

"In accepting Beth's job offer." She smiled. "Turns out I'm not so sure that it's the right path for me."

Daniel listened, joy slowly stealing upon him as she grasped her meaning. She wasn't dead-set on going. Maybe he could try and change her mind.

Dimly, in the distance, he heard someone calling his name, but he ignored it. He was too caught up in what was happening in front of him.

Amanda leaned toward him. "I was just wondering, if you had an opinion on the subject."

Daniel grinned. "Oh, I've got opinions."

"I thought you might."

There was his name again. Even Amanda noticed it this time.

She turned. "Is someone calling for you?"

There it was again. Daniel groaned. He hated to leave this moment, but he'd better see what was going on. Grabbing Amanda's hand, he pulled her to the door. "You're coming with me," he said. "You're not leaving my sight until we finish this conversation."

"Deal."

They started down the hall toward the waiting room, slowly picking up speed as Daniel noticed that it was his one of his nurses calling for him. But what made both him and Amanda start running was when a new voice entered the fray.

"Daniel!" Sarah was yelling in a terrified voice. "Daniel, I need you."

Daniel and Amanda burst into the waiting room, past a nurse who he assumed was on her way to fetch him. Sarah was standing at the door looking panic-stricken, and Daniel's blood turned cold.

"Thank God," she cried. "You've got to come help me! He's in the car."

Daniel let go of Amanda's hand and sprinted for the door. "Is it Ethan?"

"No," said Sarah. "It's Robert. I don't know what's happening. But something is really wrong."

CHAPTER 12

Amanda rushed to the car, fast on Daniel's heels. He pulled open the door and fumbled with the straps of his nephew's car seat. Amanda glanced over his head and saw enough to confirm that Robert was in serious trouble. Ethan sat his seat next to Robert. He looked confused at all the activity. Amanda dashed back inside to the waiting room, throwing what she hoped was a reassuring look at Sarah as she passed.

Inside, there were some children with their parents sitting in a corner of the room, looking worried. The three on-duty nurses were standing in a clump at the front desk, tense as they awaited instructions.

Amanda went straight to the group, giving out directions as quickly as she could think of them.

"We've got an emergency here. First, can someone please go prep the first exam room? Stay there to assist us when it's ready. We'll also need someone to call Kyle. He should be here. After that, keep an eye on any patients in the building. Let them know they might have to wait a little before Dr. Shane sees them." Amanda closed her eyes as two of the nurses hurried off. What else? "And can someone please go get Ethan out his car seat and take care of him until we've finished with Robert? Sarah needs to stay with us right now, and Ethan looks scared."

No sooner had she finished issuing directions than Daniel dashed into the building, holding a limp Robert in his arms.

"Room one," called Amanda, running behind him.

He nodded and headed for the prepared space, Sarah hurrying behind them.

Daniel positioned Robert upon the bed and immediately began listening to his heart. Amanda hurried to loosen Robert's shirt.

"His pulse has slowed," he said to Amanda.

"Look around his lips," said Amanda quietly. "He's turning blue." She stared at Daniel's stricken face. "Do you think it could be his heart?"

Daniel leaned his head out of the room door. "Someone call for life flight," he yelled in a commanding voice. "Now!"

"I'm on it," Amanda heard a nurse call. She continued examining Robert. She wrapped a blood pressure cuff on his tiny arm.

She turned to Sarah. "What were you doing before this started?" she asked as the machine began to measure his blood pressure. Daniel had joined them again and had resumed his examination.

"Playing outside," said Sarah. "Robert fell down and hurt his knee, so he was fussy, but nothing out of the ordinary. After ten minutes or so, he calmed down. I put him and Ethan in the car to get groceries. On my way to town, though —" her voice caught in her throat. "He started coughing first, and it got louder and stronger. I pulled over to make sure he was ok, and he looked awful. So I hightailed it here." She ended in a little sob. "Is he going to be ok?"

The machine attached to Robert beeped, and Amanda quickly read the output.

"Blood pressure is low," she said warningly.

"Amanda," Daniel said suddenly. "Look at this."

Amanda hurried to his side and peered at the spot he'd indicated. There, on the back of Robert's knee was a swollen red welt.

Slowly, their eyes met, and Amanda saw the same conclusion in Daniel's face that she had reached.

He'd been stung by a wasp. He was in anaphylactic shock.

Amanda froze for just a moment, memories of Steven and his allergic reaction swarming her brain. Could she do this? It was a life-or-death situation, and one mistake on her part could have the most serious consequences imaginable. How was she supposed to do this?

Stay with me, Lord, she prayed desperately. *Please, take away my fear. I can't do this alone.*

With a huge effort, she pushed her fears away. She didn't know how, but she knew that God could use her, afraid or not. And she had to act now to save Robert. Life flight wouldn't come in time.

"Get me an epi," she said to Daniel. He nodded and ran out.

She turned to the nurse. "I need Benadryl right away, and albuterol and a nebulizer if you've got it. After that, find any steroids that you have in the building and bring them to me."

Daniel was back. He had an assortment of epi-pens. Amanda knew that most doctors kept some on hand in case of an emergency. And this was certainly an emergency.

"The dose will be too strong," he said, handing her a pen. "Robert's too little."

"I know," said Amanda. She plunged the epi-pen into a box of tissues on the counter, the medicine shooting out into the interior. Daniel watched her with shock on his face, but she didn't have time to explain.

Expertly, she cracked open the end of the pen now that she had disengaged the spring. She was back in her element now. She'd never treated anyone in anaphylactic shock before who was so young, but she still knew what to do. She'd learned this trick years ago in a seminar she'd taken on emergency medicine for wilderness settings. She'd never realized how useful it would become.

She'd have to drop the seminar leader an email, she thought in passing.

Carefully, she removed the vial of medicine from inside the pen. Just as she'd expected, there was a large reserve of medicine left inside. She measured out the right amount for a child Robert's size and quickly injected it into his small thigh.

While she'd been busy with the epi-pen, the nurse had come in. She gave Robert a dose of allergy medicine and then set up the nebulizer to administer the breathing medication.

Amanda carefully pulled Robert to a sitting position and transferred him to Sarah. She directed them to a chair and then fitted Robert with a child-sized mask. The medicine started flowing through the mask, and Amanda readied another dose of medicine in the syringe in case the first wasn't enough. Sarah's arms gripped her child tightly, rocking him slightly from side to side as Daniel measured his blood pressure again.

"It's working," he said after a minute, standing with a relieved smile on his face. "Blood pressure is stabilizing. His breathing has improved."

Sarah closed her eyes. "Thank the Lord."

"Amen," said Amanda. "I think he's out of the woods, Sarah, but he still needs to be seen at the hospital."

The nurse had returned with steroids. Amanda looked through what was available. "I think we should give him this one," she said to Daniel. "It's the most fast acting, and it might help keep him stable. What do you think?"

Daniel looked seriously at her. "You're the expert here, Amanda. Whatever you say."

Amanda took a deep breath before turning to the nurse. "Please administer the correct dose to him right away."

Sarah's eyes were shining with unshed tears. "I can't thank you two enough," she said in a shaky voice.

Daniel knelt next to her and put a hand on Robert's knee. Now that the little boy could breath easily again, he smiled beneath the mask at his uncle.

"You know there isn't anything we wouldn't do for these boys, Sarah," said Daniel, and Amanda was touched his use of the word "we."

Just then they heard the front door chime jangling as the door banged open.

"Where's Robert?" they heard Kyle shout. "Where's my son?"

Daniel stuck his head back into the hallway. "Back here. He's doing great," he called. "And stop bellowing. You're going to scare the patients."

Kyle burst into the room, past Daniel, and threw his arms around Robert.

"He's going to be fine," said Sarah, putting a hand on his shoulder and dropping her head onto his. "He's going to be fine. They saved him."

Daniel put his arm around Amanda. "You saved him," he said so quietly that she almost didn't hear him.

She turned to look at him and was startled to see an expression of such love on his face that she almost kissed him right then and there. Luckily, she remembered the presence of other people in the room, including a nurse who was staring at them with undisguised interest.

"It was a team effort," she murmured.

Twenty minutes later, the crew from life flight arrived to airlift Robert to the nearest medical center, over 200 miles away. Sarah went with him, while Kyle stayed with Ethan.

Amanda and Daniel stood with Kyle and his son as they watched the helicopter take off from a nearby field. Ethan was fascinated by the helicopter. He kept pointing at the aircraft, occasionally reaching out for his like he wanted to go for a ride, too.

"So, Robert is allergic to wasps," said Kyle, shaking his head.

"Looks that way," said Daniel.

"Kids," said Kyle with a sigh. "They sure keep you on your toes."

"It's nothing you can't handle," said Daniel. "You and Sarah are so strong together. And for the times when you're not," he gave an apologetic smile, "that's what God's there for, right?"

Kyle stared at him, then turned to Amanda. "I don't know what you did to him, but keep it up."

Amanda smiled and slipped her hand into Daniel's. "I can't take credit for this one."

Just then the helicopter started to lift from the ground.

"Robert's going to be ok, right?" asked Kyle, keeping his eyes on the aircraft.

Amanda nodded. "He'll be fine. It's just always a good idea to be monitored in a case like this. He'll probably be home by tomorrow."

Kyle sighed. "Good."

They all watched quietly as the helicopter flew off, becoming smaller and smaller in the sky.

Ethan unexpectedly was the first to speak. He pointed at the retreating chopper and very clearly stated, "More."

"Hey," Kyle said in delight. "That's the first time he's said that word." He smiled tenderly at his son. "We're making progress, aren't we, buddy?"

Ethan smiled and nuzzled his head into his dad's shoulder. Then he started rubbing his eyes.

"Take that boy home," commanded Daniel. "He looks exhausted."

"That makes two of us," said Kyle. He shook Daniel's hand and gave Amanda a hug. "I'll never forget what you two did today. Never."

"Just think," said Amanda as they watched Kyle drive off, "one short year from now and you'll have the facilities here in town to treat something like this. That's going to be such a help."

Daniel turned to face her. "What you did in there was amazing."

"No, it wasn't," said Amanda coloring. "That's how you treat anaphylaxis. Anyone would have done the same."

"I'm not talking about the treatment," said Daniel, "although that was spot-on. Nor am I talking about the way you dismembered that epi-pen to get the right amount of medicine." Amanda laughed at his word choice, but Daniel stayed serious. "I'm talking about how you didn't give in to fear. Not once. You were faced with a life or death situation with a child that you know and love, and you still did what had to be done." He smiled at her. "Where's that scared doctor who rolled into town one month ago?"

Amanda sighed. "She grew up. With some help from above." She slid her arm around Daniel's back and leaned into him. "I admit, there was a moment when I almost froze. I was so scared, Daniel. I didn't know if I could see a way through it."

"What happened?" Daniel asked quietly.

She smiled. "God heard my prayer."

Together they stood arm-in-arm, savoring the moment of quiet after the drama of that day.

"It's funny," Daniel finally said, "with all the worrying we do about Ethan, it was Robert who needed lifesaving treatment. I did not see that coming."

"Life's full of surprises," said Amanda. She glanced at her watch. "Like the surprise Beth is going to get when I don't make that flight."

Daniel looked at her steadily. "Should we call her and explain? There may be time to salvage your job."

Amanda waved her hand dismissively. "What job?" She snuggled closer. "I'm right where I'm meant to be."

ONE WEEK later, Daniel picked Amanda up from her hotel in the evening.

"We've got to find you somewhere more permanent to stay," he said, opening his truck door for her.

"I know," said Amanda, climbing in. "I've just been too busy to look for a place. It seems like every kid in town picked this week to get sick."

Daniel joined her in the cab. "I'll speak to them about it," he said. "I can't have them scaring off my new partner."

She laughed. "I'm not going anywhere."

Daniel glanced at her from the corner of his eye. Ever since she'd made the decision to stay one week ago, she'd been looking so happy. She was humming at work, and he'd even caught her doing a little dance while she read patient charts. He hoped what was about to happen would make her happiness complete.

"Thanks for babysitting with me," he said. "Ever since the wasp sting, Robert's become super attached to you."

"He's such a sweetheart," Amanda said, leaning back in the seat. "They both are. I'll babysit with you anytime." She looked out the window as they drove. "Where are Sarah and Kyle going tonight?"

"Just out to dinner," said Daniel. "Nothing special. I think they needed a chance to unwind from this past week."

Amanda nodded. "They have been through a lot." She stretched her arms out. "I'm looking forward to some baby snuggle time."

After a few more minutes, they pulled up to the house, and Amanda frowned to see how dark everything was.

"What's going on?" Amanda asked. "It looks like no one's home."

They knocked on the front door. When no one answered the first or second knocks, Daniel tried the door. "It's locked."

"You're sure it was tonight?" she asked.

"Positive." Daniel looked around. "Maybe they're out back?" he suggested.

"That's weird," said Amanda. "It's late to be hanging in the backyard." Still, she allowed Daniel to lead her around to the side of the house.

When they turned the corner, Amanda gasped and froze.

Daniel grinned. He'd expected her reaction, but it was no less enjoyable to really see it.

Ahead of them, the gazebo had been completely covered with white lights. It shone in the gathering darkness like a fairy tent.

Daniel gently led Amanda forward, bringing her onto the wood planking underneath the lights. "Don't worry," he whispered playfully, "Kyle cleared the last of the wasps."

He watched her climb the gazebo steps, her face full of wonder and delight.

"Do you like it?" he asked with a smile.

"Did – did you do this?" she asked, her eyes wide.

"I'd do a lot more for you," said Daniel. He held her hands and turned to face her. "I wish I could put into words how much you mean to me, Amanda. I love you, and I will go on loving you for the rest of my life."

He was surprised to hear a catch in his voice, but he pressed on.

"I never thought that God would so bless me with someone like you. You are the woman for me."

Slowly, he dropped to one knee and pulled out the ring he'd been hiding in his pocket. Amanda's eyes grew even wider, and her mouth fell open.

"Amanda Garvas, will you marry me?"

For one terrifying breath of a second, Amanda didn't speak. Then her look of shock transformed into one of complete and utter joy.

"Of course I'll marry you," she cried.

Sure that he was grinning like a fool, Daniel slipped the ring onto her finger. It picked up all the lights and reflected them back merrily, matching his feelings exactly.

Jumping to his feet, Daniel drew Amanda to him in a joyful kiss.

"I will never let you go," he growled, as the kiss ended.

"You'd better not," she said, her eyes twinkling. She held him tightly around the neck and stared into his eyes. "I love you, Daniel. I can't imagine a life without you by my side."

"You don't have to," he whispered. Drawn in by her eyes again, he kissed her, filling the embrace with all his hopes and dreams for their future together. She responded in kind, and Daniel thought he could feel the blessings of God Himself descending upon them.

He finally lifted his head minutes later to the sound of celebration. He turned and saw Sarah, Kyle, and the boys. Both Sarah and Kyle were cheering and even the boys seemed to know something special was going on as they banged their hands together.

"She said yes," he called, still holding tight to Amanda.

"We gathered that," said Kyle. The family ran up the steps to hug Daniel and Amanda.

Daniel looked at Amanda being embraced by his family, her face a state of joyous confusion, and he felt happier than he ever had before.

"Where were you guys?" demanded Amanda.

"Hiding inside," said Sarah. "Daniel gave us strict orders to not come out too early."

"So, we're not really babysitting?" she asked, looking almost disappointed.

Everyone laughed.

"Not tonight," said Kyle, "but we promise to use you shamelessly in the future."

"That's right," said Sarah. "The boys can't get enough of their Aunt Amanda."

Amanda met Daniel's eyes. "I'm Aunt Amanda?"

Daniel pulled her to him in another fierce hug. "Of course you are," he murmured. "It's about time you had an official place in the family, to match the place you already hold in my heart."

EPILOGUE

All of Highland Canyon turned out for the day that turned their one-Dr. Shane town into a two-Dr. Shane town.

Amanda was a radiant bride, set off perfectly by the loving support of her two bridesmaids, Millie and Sarah. Daniel stood with Kyle as his best man, and, in their father's arms, Robert and Ethan made two of the most adorable ring bearers the town had ever seen.

The love and peace exuded by the bride and groom was evident to all, and even Ernie was known to wipe away a tear during their vows to each other.

At the end of the ceremony, the minister smiled and announced, "Introducing for the first time, the two Dr. Shanes!" The crowd broke out into riotous applause as Daniel and Amanda met for a joyful kiss. Secure in their trust first in God and then in each other, they clasped hands and grinned at one another as they walked down the aisle.

ONE YEAR after their marriage, the new medical center was up and running. Daniel was very busy with his practice and was able to offer services at the new clinic that he'd only dreamed of before. Robert and Ethan were frequent visitors to Uncle Daniel's, as Ethan had begun physical therapy. His parents and aunt and uncle watched him with pride as he grew stronger every day. Daniel continued to offer once-a-month art days, and the event started drawing children from all over the region.

Amanda was a resident at the new medical center as well as its administrator. The first task she set for herself was to recruit new talent to the staff. In the short time that the center had been open, she'd successfully recruited top speech and occupational therapists to the center, and she was in talks with a young surgeon out of Portland. She divided what was left of her time between treating her own patient load and overseeing the medical students from Washington State, a group who had been invaluable in meeting the demand for services. She corresponded frequently with Beth Weisman to keep her apprised of the state of the clinic, and the two had gone back to being on friendly terms.

Dr. Kowalski visited the center soon after it opened. She toured the facility with Amanda and Daniel, exclaiming over the new equipment and layout. Her seal of approval meant the world to both Amanda and Daniel. They knew it was only her unwavering faith in them that had made the project a reality.

ONE SUMMER evening after a particularly busy day, Amanda slipped out of the clinic. She dropped into the diner quickly before heading to her husband's practice. She found him hard at work in his office, just as she'd expected.

He looked up when she came through the door, a brilliant smile lighting his features. "Hello, stranger," he said, pushing his work away.

"Hello, yourself," said Amanda, coming to his side. "Are you busy?"

Daniel put his arms around her waist and pulled her down onto his lap. She laughed as she fell and steadied herself by putting her arms around his neck.

"Never too busy for you," said Daniel.

"Good," said Amanda, wiggling her eyebrows. "Because I've made us a picnic."

"A picnic?"

"What?" Amanda gave him a spirited look. "You think you're the only one who can pack picnics? I'll have you know Millie will supply me with food as well as you."

"What did I do to get saddled with such a sassy woman?" asked Daniel, before he brought his lips to hers in one long kiss.

When he finally lifted his head, he looked dazed.

"What were we talking about?"

Amanda laughed. "A picnic." She stood and pulled him to his feet. "Come on. I want to go before it gets dark."

Daniel laughed. "You know we're not going to meet any wolves."

"You never know," said Amanda.

"You can take the girl out of Seattle..." murmured Daniel, but he followed her with a smile.

They rode out in blissful silence, Amanda sitting with her head on Daniel's shoulder, enjoying the rolling Montana hills in the company of the man she loved.

When they finally reached the location of their very first picnic, they walked out to the edge of the rock gorge. Daniel set the basket down in what they'd come to think of as their spot.

Amanda spread out a blanket, and the two began to enjoy the delicious meal packed for them by Millie.

"You know," said Amanda, "we may not be able to come out here for a while. We'd better enjoy it while it lasts."

"What do you mean?" asked Daniel, dividing a large apple pie slice into two pieces for sharing.

"It's a rough trail here. I'm not sure we're going to want to make it with a stroller."

"A stroll —" Daniel froze. "Did you say a stroller?"

Amanda nodded, sure that her joy must be showing in every part of her face.

Daniel gave out a whoop and wrapped his arms around her.

"You're really pregnant?" he asked. "We're having a baby?"

"We're having a baby," whispered Amanda.

"Praise God!" he shouted. Then he kissed Amanda reverently, starting with her forehead, her cheeks, her lips, and ending with the tips of all ten of her fingers.

Then they sat together, their bodies pressed side-by-side as they looked out over the ravine. The late afternoon sun sent streaks of orange and pink across the sky, and nearby some birds trilled at the ending of the day.

"Daniel," said Amanda. "I have to admit, I'm a little nervous."

Daniel chuckled. "Good. Because I am, too."

"Really?"

"Really."

Amanda sighed. "I feel like we have no idea what we're getting into."

"Probably no parent does. But you know what?"

"What?" asked Amanda, leaning into her husband's strong shoulder.

"God hasn't let us down yet. We will just have to trust Him."